Only a Lower Paradise

and Other Stories

Only a Lower Paradise
and Other Stories

Michael Bryson

BOHEME PRESS

Toronto

Edited by Max Maccari and Andrea Foley
Text and page design by Patricia Cipolla @ Magpie Media

Canadian Cataloguing in Publication Data

Bryson, Michael, 1968 –
Only a lower paradise and other stories

Short Stories
ISBN 1-894498-15-1

I. Title.

PS8553.R97O54 2000   C813'.54   C00-932072-5
PR9199.3.B744O54 2000

Previous versions of these stories have appeared in the following
magazines: "Only a Lower Paradise" (Chapter 6) as "Heresy" (*The Hart
House Review*); "Gerry" (*Blood & Aphorisms*); "Waiting for a Miracle" (*The
New Quarterly*); "American Beauty" as "Bike Tricks" (*The New Quarterly*);
"Once Upon a Time" (*Voices Under the Guise of Darkness*); "Crow Teaches
City Boy a Few Tricks" (*Front and Centre Magazine*)

Boheme Press
P.O. Box 1017, Station F
Toronto, Ontario, Canada M4Y 2T7
www.bohemeonline.com

For Crow

Contents

Love and wonder, then, are stages in an imaginative expansion: they establish a permanent unity of subject and object, and they lift us from a world of subject and object to a world of lover and beloved. Yet they afford us only a lower Paradise after all . . . The highest possible state, therefore, is not the union of lover and beloved, but of creator and creature, of energy and form. This latter is the state for which Blake reserves the name Eden.

— Northrop Frye, *Fearful Symmetry*

ᚳ

All Bibles or sacred codes have been the causes of the following Errors:

1. That Man has two real existing principles; Viz.: a Body & a soul.
2. That Energy, calld Evil, is alone from the Body, & that Reason, calld Good, is alone from the Soul.
3. That God will torment Man in Eternity for following his Energies.

But the following Contraries to these are True:

1. Man has no Body distinct from his Soul; for that called Body is a portion of Soul discernd by the five Senses, the chief inlets of Soul in this age.
2. Energy is the only life, and is from the Body; and Reason is the bound or outward circumference of Energy.
3. Energy is Eternal Delight.

— William Blake, *The Marriage of Heaven and Hell*

Only a Lower Paradise

CHAPTER 1

Late one fateful day, the sun sinking but still warm in the sky, Martha, my guardian angel, was late. God was dead, and Heaven was in a tizzy. One of Lucifer's agents had broken the news, uncovering a vast conspiracy at the highest levels of the cosmic order. For three hundred, possibly four hundred years, God's death had been kept a secret. Gabriel was said to be a ringleader, closely aligned with the Holy Ghost. Who had led the cover-up was a major source of rumour, though Richard Nixon was sure to be named. It was uncertain at that time whether Jesus would be implicated. *The Galactic Times* reported he had been away for the past half-century on a fact-finding mission to another dimension, and had not yet returned.

Now that I think about it, the previous time I had seen Martha she had seemed distracted, which was strange, since angels were supposed to be perfect. I remember she told me about the problems she was having finding a set of replacement wings and how her halo had started to fade.

I had a hard time imagining Martha with a halo and wings since she always showed up in my bedroom wearing trackpants and a tanktop. She certainly was perfect, though. Once when we went walking along Venice Beach we were stopped by this guy who said he was a photographer for the *Sports Illustrated* swimsuit issue. He begged Martha to let him photograph her in the surf, but Martha pulled a used copy of *The Second Sex* out of her handbag and told him to do some reading. That's how Martha dealt with problems: she pulled the solution out of her handbag. I've seen more than a dozen genuine miracles, a million times more impressive than that book episode, emerge out of that tattered piece of cotton cloth.

The week before she was late she visited me after attending a meeting on the natural re-alignment of the cosmos — an event that took place every twenty billion years. She said I was lucky to be alive, though most of the action was taking place on the other side of the universe. On Earth the stars would probably twinkle about fifty per cent brighter for approximately a week, which in retrospect is an incredibly general statement for an angel to make. They are very keen on numbers, and they are supposedly never wrong. This is why God decided to break the barrier that had existed between Heaven and Earth since the beginning of time, sending angels to the surface of the planet to meddle directly in human affairs. Things had gotten out of control. Things needed to be straightened out. And since angels were perfect . . . but I suppose it wasn't God who had broken the cosmic membrane. Besides, things weren't really any worse than they had ever been.

It was ten years ago, right after that whole Y2K fixation, when the first angel appeared openly on Earth. A being calling himself *Extreme*, complete with twenty-foot wings and a glowing aura, materialized over a crowd of screaming adolescents packed into Madison Square Garden to see aging pop star Madonna's "Middle-Aged and Frisky" Reunion Tour. The pop star was in the middle of her simulated "Like a Virgin" masturbation sequence when *Extreme* boomed, "THE WALLS ARE COMING DOWN," and exploded in a flash of light and rubber, spraying lubricated condoms across the floor and into the first and second sections of the stands. Madonna credited her special effects crew, who denied all knowledge of the event.

Two days later, Elijah and Moses walked into the Vatican and demanded an audience with the Pope. They told his Holiness that *Extreme* was Satan's agent. The opening of the cosmic membrane had yet to be fine-tuned to prevent the Devil from taking advantage of it. The Pope thanked them, and after posing for photographs with the two members of the Old Testament Hall of Fame, he was spirited off to Heaven for a tête-à-tête with the Commander-in-Chief.

Apparently though, that meeting never took place, since the Pope had yet to return and God, we were told, was dead.

The day Martha was late, she materialized in my closet — her favourite place for materializing — walked over to my bed, and curled up into a shivering ball. She pulled her knees to her chest, dropped her head into her lap, and began trembling. I offered her a blanket, but she refused it and motioned for me to fetch her a coffee.

When I returned with a steaming cup of cappuccino, she was in the shower, singing the Twenty-Third Psalm.

A note was on the bed.

MEMORANDUM

To: Guardian Angels
From: Supreme Cosmic Command
Re: Cosmic Re-organization
Date: July 12, 2012

The purpose of this memo is to inform you that the time has come to involve your clients in the cosmic re-organization.

As you are in no doubt aware, the cosmic re-organization is a primary objective of the

Supreme Cosmic Command. The role your clients will play is of the utmost importance. You must begin securing your objectives within the next three Earth days. All objectives must be secured within the month.

We understand that as a result of recent announcements made in the Cosmic Press and information leaked by certain underworld authorities, many of you have had a more difficult time than usual dealing with your caseloads. We are sympathetic to your concerns, but we must also stress that the future of the cosmos depends on the success of this operation.

If we can help you in any way to secure the eternal freedom of the universe, please let us know.

"Jonathan, you shouldn't be reading that," Martha scolded.

"What is it?" I asked.

"What does it look like?"

"What does it mean, *clients*?"

"It means you, silly."

"I thought we were friends."

"Oh, sure. That, too."

Martha pulled a pack of cigarettes out of her Bag of Miracles, lit one, lifted her head to look at me, and let out a long, deep sigh.

"Martha, what's going on?" I asked.

Martha ignored me and stared at the ceiling.

When she first began visiting me, Martha told me everything. She told me why the sky was blue, why the world was round, why the geo-political realities of the twenty-first century had necessitated an unprecedented break in the cosmic continuum. It was an exciting time. The possibilities seemed endless. But then, as it always happens, patterns began to form, and we became a little bored with each other, then a little more bored, then, in the end, really, really bored. That's when we began asking the "significant questions." We began discussing the rumours that there was trouble inside the Cosmic Palace, and how God was preparing a shakedown of Heaven's high-ranking officials. Martha told me everything she knew about Heaven, and I told her everything I knew about Earth. Together we realized we knew very little, since we could always think of questions the other couldn't answer. Lately, however, we were not making any progress in our question-and-answer game.

"What's the memo about, Martha?"

"I don't know."

"What do you mean you don't know?"

"I don't understand what the memo means by *objectives*."

"Things you need to achieve."

"They told us the cosmic re-alignment was a natural phenomena; it would happen as a matter of consequence. At first, we weren't supposed to do anything more than inform people that it was taking place — to allow them to understand another small part of the mysteries of the cosmos. Then, all of a sudden, it was a political priority, and what had been a re-alignment became a re-organization."

Martha began pacing the room.

"I don't think I want to be an angel anymore," she said. "I don't think I like being an angel."

"Martha!"

"I'm so tired, Jon. I'm so sick and tired of being someone the cosmic planners move around like a checker piece across the board; except checker pieces have more freedom than angels. Angels are robots, conformists, reactionaries. I never knew

17

anything about doubt until I met you, Jon. I never knew anything about betrayal until they announced God was dead. Then I began to wonder what I had been doing with myself since the beginning of time. For all of eternity, I've been someone else's tool. Now I want to do something for myself. I want to be free."

It was at this moment that I suddenly realized Martha was less than perfect. Uncertainty was a distinctly human trait. Maybe she didn't know everything about Heaven, but I had always thought she understood how things fit together, the order and the hierarchy of existence. I suddenly understood. Martha was as close to the ultimate cosmic design as I was to the Oval Office. I used to think angels knew everything. I had thought they understood the purpose of every speck of dust, every grain of sand. I thought every grain of sand had a purpose. There had been a very large and successful movement at the end of the twentieth century to prove the idea of purpose was anachronistic. Purpose was something people gave themselves. Anything meaningful was circumstantial. If every grain of sand had a purpose, it was because people gave the grains that purpose — not because the sand had any purpose essential to itself. This is the sort of thing the angels had originally come to dispute, refute, and destroy: to cure the existential angst that had settled over the populous.

The first time I met Martha I was half-way through watching my copy of Wrestlemania XVI when she interrupted the television circuit to inform me I was about to become a privileged member of a Priority One Experiment of the Supreme Cosmic Command. I would be receiving counselling from an angel. Her name was Martha. She would help me sort out all my metaphysical problems — and a couple of physical ones as well. I was to expect my first visitation within the next thirty seconds. Please put some coffee on.

Well, I thought. There's something new.

And then, after I poured the water into the coffee-maker and settled back into my chair to watch the grand finale, there she was, in trackpants, sandals, and tanktop, her blond hair held back with an elastic, her high cheek bones, flushed face, and sparkling blue eyes fully exposed in all their brilliance.

"Hi," she said.

"Hi."

"I'm Martha."

"Right."

From there we built a relationship that has been by far the most significant in my life. Martha showed me life can be meaningful, if you have the right approach, and I did my best to show her that things are not always what they seem.

"Jon," she said, almost crying. "What are we going to do?"

"There's only one thing to do," I said. "Go on the road."

Martha looked at me blankly.

"I'll call Robert. We'll be in Denver by the weekend, New York by the middle of next week. If we don't get messed up with something in between, that is."

Robert used to be my neighbour in Venice Beach before he moved to San Francisco. He was my buddy in college. We used to drink to excess together, tell each other our fantasies, cheat on each other while playing poker. Robert was excellent at marking cards. Two years ago, Robert married Che-Maria, a Spanish woman he had met at the race track. Robert was there to place a couple of hundred dollars on a horse in the fifth race. Che-Maria was there to pick the patron's pockets. She was an illegal immigrant and picking pockets was her only means of gainful employment. When she tried to pick Robert's pocket, Robert's pet mouse, Herbert, bit her, and she had to be rushed to the hospital. On the way there, in the back of the ambulance, Robert and Che-Maria fell in love.

"But Jon," Martha wondered. "What about the Supreme Cosmic Command? If they find out I've deserted, they'll banish me to Hell. And they'll kill you and banish your soul there, too."

"We're all going to die someday," I said.

"This is something I have never experienced," Martha replied.

So I called Robert, and he said he would be at my front door first thing the next day, his van loaded down with a three-week supply of canned goods, toilet paper, and bug repellent. I told him we wanted to go on a camping trip. Robert loved to camp, and he was anxious to meet Martha, he said, though he didn't know she was an angel.

CHAPTER 2

Martha and Robert and I set out from Venice Beach in Robert's van with three week's worth of canned beans and bacon. Our plan was to stop briefly in San Francisco, where we would pick up Che-Maria, and head over the mountains for Denver.

I had not been outside of Venice Beach since I had graduated from a small liberal arts college in Oregon five years earlier.

Robert and I were a real pair in those days. We would spend our nights refining our poker game, every once in a while coercing some of the other guys in our dorm into a round for serious cash, which usually presented us with beer money for the next two weeks. Our days were spent drifting from poetry seminars to computer workshops.

I had a girlfriend, too. Pique. A fine arts major. She specialized in graphic design. I still have some of the photographs she took of me and Robert and the rest of our crowd. Mostly experimental stuff, very weird. In one collage she had my head attached to the body of President Quayle.

Pique came into my life in a strange way. She was taking a course in Modern American Literature and a mutual friend told her I knew something about Hemingway — which was a laugh. All I knew about Hemingway was that he was dead and had once had a thing about bullfights. That's all I remember my high school English teacher saying about him. We had read a short story out of an anthology, and the teacher had gone on about how bullfights were symbolic of the Hemingway Hero, a noble man struggling against significant odds. It was farcical, really. But that's what people went for in those days, I guess. Machismo. Real blood and guts stuff. Earthy. In the end it got Hemingway, too. Blew his head off with a shotgun. None of which I told Pique. I just asked her what she wanted to know, and she said, "Oh, you know, just enough to get this essay finished. Why don't you come back to my apartment?" So I did, and for the next three years, for reasons I have yet to understand — though not for lack of trying — we were lovers, through many growing pains and countless pleasures.

When Martha first started visiting me, I was real depressed. Pique had come back from a European vacation three months before and moved in with a sculptor she met on a train in Germany. We hadn't planned on getting married or anything; it's just that I was beginning to think I might love her. I know that's a stupid thing to say, but for better or worse it's the closest explanation I can come up with that even vaguely resembles the truth.

Martha said I was right; it was a vague explanation, and she told me I had been wrong to take my relationship with Pique for granted. I still miss her, though. Sometimes I miss her one-hell-of-a-lot. I miss Che-Maria, too. When Robert and Martha and I pulled into their driveway in San Francisco and Che-Maria came bombing out of the house with hugs and kisses for everyone, I suddenly remembered how much.

"Jon, Jon, Jon," she squealed. "You must see my new toaster. It holds four pieces of bread at once."

She was crazy about appliances, having never had any when she lived on the streets and no television to tell her what she was missing. She was at quite a loss when Robert brought her back to the suburbs after her short stay in the hospital to recover from the mouse bite. In the six months before she met Robert, she had only worn clothes she had stolen from Salvation Army dumpsters. All the belongings she had brought with her across the border in the back of a farmer's pickup truck were lost when the farmer took an unexpectedly short rest at a truck stop. More than once Che-Maria had cursed herself that she had never learned the quickest way to pee.

She dressed in fashion now and was well-versed on all the latest style trends, but kitchen appliances were another universe altogether. They were an endless source of amusement for her. She couldn't get over how shiny they were.

"Che-Maria," I said. "This is Martha."

"Oh, Martha. Yes. Robert told me Jon had a new girlfriend. You are very pretty. She is very pretty, Jon. Now both of you come inside and see my new toaster. I'll make some toast for you. It's very good, and quick."

"Nice to meet you," said Martha, quickly adding, "I'd love some toast, thanks."

Che-Maria led Martha across the manicured lawn, around the over-populated flower beds, and under the Corinthian arch set into her and Robert's modest suburban bungalow. Modest, of course, in a relative California kind of way.

I started to follow them, but Robert grabbed my arm and directed me around the side of the house to the backyard.

"OK, champ," he said. "Who's the babe?"

"Martha?"

"Yeah, man. Who else?"

"I met her at the beach." I lied.

"Yeah?"

"She just came up to me and asked if I hadn't been in her class at UCLA." This was the story Martha and I had invented.

"What did you say?"

"I said yes, of course."

"Good, man. Excellent style." Robert was hip on style. "What next?"

"She started talking about some Professor Larson, and I agreed with everything she said. Larson was a bumbler and a fool. His lessons were catastrophic free-for-alls, and nobody had a clue going into the exam what the questions would be like. Sounds like some of our profs, huh?"

"Yeah."

"Then she told me she had gone to this Larson guy to ask about her term paper, and he had suggested they go for a coffee to talk about it."

"Ah." Robert was so gullible.

"She had just broken it off with Larson when she picked me up. She probably thought she had found somebody who would understand what she had been through."

"She's gorgeous, man. And a lot more stable than that Pique chick."

I hated myself for lying to Robert, particularly for making Martha seem ordinary, but Martha had been insistent no one find out she was an angel. As long as we kept a low profile, we would be alright, she said. While God knew and saw everything, there was no equivalent power in Heaven at the moment. That's why the Supreme Cosmic Command was so nervous about their agents securing their objectives. The situation was in serious risk of destabilizing, and they had no way of controlling it if it did. The plan of the Supreme Cosmic Command was to place angel agents in key positions of power: to replace all heads of state, all advertising executives, and the leading point-getters of all the professional sports leagues. Television executives, newspaper editors, and late-night talk show hosts were secondary objectives, followed by church officials and academic deans.

"But Martha," I had asked her then, "Why can't things just go on as they always have?"

"Things are not improving," she said.

"According to whose schedule? I think that's a load of bafflegab, myself."

"Well," she said. "That's what you humans are good at — independent thought. But what do you know about the cosmic continuum? What do you know about running the universe?"

"Still," I said. "I don't see how this so-called crisis warrants all this intervention."

This was the sort of argument I had with Martha every once in a while, and it never turned out well. She would never give in because she had never been wrong in the history of the universe, although something inside her told her she might be this time.

"Nice pool, Rob," I said, once we had reached the backyard. "Can we go for a swim after lunch?"

"Hey, yeah. We'll have to try and get that girlfriend of yours into a bikini."

Che-Maria poked her head out the back door.

"Your toast is ready, Jon," she said, smiling.

Che-Maria was always smiling. She found goodness in everything. Nothing irked her except the most overt forms of violence, cruelty, and oppression, which made her extremely susceptible to the political and commercial propaganda that played on people's emotions and their intuition against things wrong.

"Come, Jon. Quick," she insisted. "Before it gets cold." She disappeared inside.

Soon we were sitting around Robert's and Che-Maria's kitchen. Shiny appliances littering the counters. The walls were plastered with Mickey Mouse wallpaper. The refrigerator hummed loudly. Martha sat smoking, listening to some Spanish language station playing soothing siesta music. After we finished our toast, Robert leaned forward, placed both elbows on the

25

table, and announced he had some important news to tell us before we left that afternoon.

"Quiet everyone, please," he said. "We have a problem."

We sat hushed in anticipation.

Robert had worked for the post office ever since college, struggling his way up to district manager in charge of distribution within five years. He had started at the bottom, sweeping the mail room floor, and graduated to mail-sorter-guy, mail-delivery-guy, and finally, mail-guy-who-drives-the-truck — a variation of mail-delivery-guy but more prestigious because you get your assistant to battle the Dobermans.

Robert was the fastest promoted employee in the history of his branch. In fact, he was due for another promotion. He had told me he had applied for the Director's job in the Special Deliveries Division, Government Services. It was only a matter of days.

"Yesterday, just after you called, Jon, my boss, the Director General, called me into his office and told me he was going to give me a tour of the Special Deliveries Division, which is usually off-limits to anyone but the people who work there. I had never seen it, even though I had been working in that same building every day for the past five years. I walked over to his office. We took the elevator to the basement, showed our passes to the security guards, went through two electronically-coded steel doors, and ended up in a warehouse-sized room full of robots and computers. Every couple of seconds a computer would beep and print out a message; a robot would grab the message, stuff it in an envelope, and rush across the room to drop it in a mail bag. The Director General told me the Director of Special Deliveries didn't have to do much except call the computer-repair guy. The only thing the Director could not do was read any of the messages. Then he turned his back and I picked up a message off the floor."

"Now, Jon," he said. "You know me. I'm not one to question authority, so why I broke a rule just as soon as it had passed through my ears I'll never know. But once I had done it, I couldn't undo it. Still, even after I had picked up the message, I didn't intend to read it."

"What did it say?" Martha interjected.

"It said: *Oval Office secure. CIA, FBI next. Pass it on.*"

God, I thought. It's started already.

Robert continued. "Usually I don't care about stuff like this, so long as I get paid, you know, but for some reason I felt I had to do something about this. I felt like I should take some action, but it's been such a long time since I've acted from conscience. So, anyway, I stole it."

"You what!" Che-Maria screamed.

She was such a moral person, especially for someone who's had such a rough time of life. Robert, on the other hand, who'd had a life as easy as they come, was a great relativist, usually balancing the scales in his own self-interest.

"Yeah," he said. "I thought, 'Well, this is interesting. Why don't I take it'? So I did. Now I'm in big trouble. I'll never get another promotion. I don't even know what it means!"

I looked over at Martha who had turned towards me. She shook her head.

"Don't worry, Rob," I said, trying to reassure him. "I'm sure they'll never miss it. Computer malfunction." Right. "The robot broke down. I mean, what was it doing on the floor in the first place?"

Robert picked up the keys to the van and pointed towards the door. "I just wanted you to know that," he said. "I just wanted you to know that if they're after me, we may be in for more than a camping trip."

"I don't believe a word of it," Martha said, sharply, but her eyes seemed duller and she slouched a little in her chair.

Che-Maria squirmed.

Said Martha: "I can't wait to pitch our tent, stroll down to the lake, and dive into its cool, slow, shimmering blueness." Angels can be so poetic.

Said Robert: "I can't wait to get the hell out of here."

CHAPTER 3

Like I said, Robert loved to camp, and though I had originally conceived my life on the road as a travelling experience — drifting through nameless Mid-Western towns, talking about nothing in particular with indescript locals, checking out foreign arcades for games I had yet to play — I was beginning to turn on to the idea of three weeks in amongst the trees. Even Martha, who had really wanted to see New York, was happy to be headed off to the woods.

Outside of San Francisco we turned north and pointed our van of renegades towards a dense pocket of redwoods that was Robert's favorite retreat.

Even before college, Robert was big on nature. His father used to take him out into the wilderness and teach him survival techniques. He knew all the right plants to eat and which ones were poisonous. He even knew how to make trail signs so you could leave messages for the campers who would follow you, and how to interpret various natural phenomena like broken branches or overturned earth so you would know if you were about to come upon a fawn and doe, or be eaten by a grizzly bear.

During the trip out of town, Martha was pensive. She sat in the back of the van wrapped in one of Robert's thick cotton camping blankets and stared out of the back window. I moved out of the front seat I was sharing with Che-Maria and snuggled up beside Martha in the back, pushing aside a couple of stray pots and pans and some loose tent pegs.

"It's starting, Jon," Martha said, hesitantly.

"I know."

"No, you don't."

"I think I know."

"That's right."

It was the fault of all humans, Martha said, to feign knowledge. When people touched truth — and each person was only offered a grain in a lifetime — they got really excited. Unfortunately, if they were the least neurotic, this grain of truth would erode what was left of their sanity, and make their lives living examples of the danger of divine revelation. Some people even said they had talked to God, when as we all know the only messengers of divine revelations are angels. Martha was constantly reminding me of the limitations of my knowledge. As an angel she knew what was true and what only seemed to be true, though her decision to quit the angel corps had left her with room for reasonable doubt on a number of matters.

What Robert's message had meant, apparently, wasn't one of them.

"They'll be after us." Martha stared at me pointedly.

I shrugged. "I know."

"Do you?"

"Yes."

"And what do you propose to do about it?"

I paused.

"Recite them the Beatitudes?" Martha chirped. "Jon, I don't think you understand. These angels, or people, or people and angels, whatever, are serious. They're deadly serious."

"I can imagine."

I looked into her face, but she turned away and became quiet again.

"I wonder if this is the Apocalypse?" she said.

This is something I had been wondering myself, but the thought of the moon turning to blood seemed somehow less scary than being confronted by members of the Supreme Cosmic Command's elite guard. Or for that matter a couple of quacks from the FBI. Or worse, a phalanx of self-styled commandos from the Internal Disciplinary Squad of the Federal Postal Service.

Che-Maria broke the tension.

"Sandwiches?" She peered back at us, smiling again. "Who wants sandwiches?"

I was famished and reached and took a pair of thick slices of country whole wheat loaf stuffed full of egg salad from Che-Maria's outstretched hand, but Martha deferred. Che-Maria wrinkled her brows and looked deeply at Martha.

"Martha," she said. "You look pale. You'll eat tuna."

I took the sandwich and placed it beside Martha, but she never ate it. Instead, she lay her head on my shoulder and slept all the way deep into the redwood trees, a revelation for me because I had never seen Martha sleep. She had been up all of the previous night pacing the house.

A couple of hours outside of San Francisco, Robert pulled off of the highway, leading us into the hinterland along an old logging road that had been abandoned for more than twenty years. The road cut a path through one of the few "forgotten" wildernesses left in California — forgotten probably more for the lack of a significant population in the area to support any kind of tax base than anything else. At the time, the loggers were waiting another ten years before they came back and cut everything down again. Since the last time Robert had brought me here, the trees had grown to hang their branches in an arch over the road. The thickened underbrush intruded in our vision. Robert ploughed the van through a sea of twigs and leaves, sending greenery flying in every direction, the side of the van being scraped by low-hanging branches.

Che-Maria began to talk about her childhood in Mexico.

"When we were kids, me and my brothers, we used to think, ah, yes, it must be wonderful to be a rich American. We thought we could have a car, two cars, three cars, and each a separate bedroom. We were four children and all slept in the same tiny room on only two mattresses."

She turned to look at Martha. "Asleep?" she whispered.

I nodded, and she continued.

"But now I know it's not so good to be a rich American."

Robert coughed, cringing. He was a red-blooded patriot. Che-Maria looked at him, saying, "Now I know we were happy children, even though we had nothing. Even though my parents had no car, no computer, no kitchen appliances, we were happy — "

Robert was becoming noticeably agitated.

"Aren't you happy?" he interrupted. "Don't you have everything you want? Don't you get everything you ask for?"

"It's true," Che-Maria admitted, her words calm in the face of Robert's disruption. "I do, and yet I still complain. Robert says I'm just a complainer. Are you happy, Jon?"

Though most people thought Che-Maria was bubble-headed, I was sure she was aware of a lot more than people gave her credit for. Was I happy? Robert — my closest friend and life-long pal — thought I was. Che-Maria, who I had only known as a passing acquaintance, was smart enough to ask, sensing I wasn't.

Martha, my guardian angel, knew the truth.

The fact was, I didn't really know myself. That's why I needed Martha. After my relationship with Pique folded, I was depressed, sure, but I felt much better now that I had been seeing Martha. I just wasn't sure if feeling better meant being happy. I wondered if I had ever really been happy. What was happy? What was there to be happy about? It was questions like these that drove me to be a recluse.

I liked my house. I didn't want to go outside. I got a job stuffing envelopes at home for a mail order company. The money paid the rent and kept me in beer, so I didn't worry too much if I wasn't doing anything with my life. What was there to do anyway? Everything people did appeared senseless to me. I started writing a book: *The Lonely Days of a Weathered Mannequin*. I thought I could explain to everybody why what they were doing was senseless, but after a couple of chapters I thought even the book was senseless, so I put it away. Meeting Martha really saved me. She got me interested in mysteries again. She piqued my curiosity, though I hate saying it that way.

I smiled at Che-Maria.

"I'm very happy," I said. "Very happy to be here with all of you."

Che-Maria leaned over and kissed me on the cheek.

"See," said Robert. "Everything's cool. We're all fine. It's those other dudes we have to worry about."

We rounded a corner and pulled out onto the beach of a lake. Martha awoke as we pulled up twenty feet short of the water.

"Yippee!" screamed Robert. "There you go Martha, there's your cool, shimmering blueness. Wow!" And he raced down to the water, threw off his clothes, and wearing only his underpants, he splashed into the shallow waves and dove into Martha's poem.

"Jon, man. C'mon!" Robert pitched. "The water's great!"

Che-Maria was already gathering stones to build a fireplace.

"Go, Jon," she said. "We'll take care of setting up."

I looked at Martha, who had rolled out of the back of the van and was beginning to search through the gear for tent poles and her Ray Bans, which had somehow fallen out of her Bag of

Miracles. She shrugged and motioned me towards the water. I hesitated but began stripping. It wasn't that I didn't want to go swimming; I just knew if I went into the water Martha would make some comment later about the women doing all the work, which was true. Robert never thought twice about the division of labour in his marriage. He brought home the money, drove the van, bought the appliances. Che-Maria did the cooking, the washing, the scraping, and the cleaning. Of course, I couldn't find my way around a kitchen until I tried to hold a surprise birthday party for Pique. Some surprise. By the time she arrived, there was flour all over the house, and the place reeked of burnt cake. Since then though, I had made huge strides in my culinary talents. In fact, when Martha started seeing me one of the first things she had me do was sign up for a cooking course. It improved my self-esteem to no end.

The water was great, and I swam out into the middle of the lake, looking back only once. I felt I had made my great escape.

They couldn't catch me now. I was gone.

Martha and Che-Maria had already set up one of the tents and had a fire burning — boiling water for Martha's coffee. Robert followed me out into the lake, but when he saw the rushes he splashed over there in search of frogs and crayfish. I could see him crawling about on his hands and knees, lunging into the lilypads every minute or so, swearing each time when he came up with nothing.

I was beginning to feel blissful and began wondering if this wasn't happiness when I started to get a cramp in my leg and decided I had better swim for shore. The sky was beginning to dull, anyway. The bugs were coming out, and a thousand gnats were swirling like a hurricane above my head. The trees swayed lightly in the slow breeze. The water was so warm.

After I had dried myself with the blanket Che-Maria had placed beside my discarded clothes, I walked up to the fire, high on the beach, where Martha offered me a steaming mug of fresh coffee.

"Leave the women to do the work, I see," she said.

"I knew you'd get me sooner or later," I replied.

She laughed, and I was glad she was feeling better.

"Hey, sport." Robert marched up the beach, jovial. "You deserted me. I could have drowned in that frog pit. Stick with your buddy, remember?"

"No chance, man," I said. "You're a fish."

"No excuse. You have to be prepared for everything." He tweaked me on the cheek. "Especially these days."

Martha handed him a mug of coffee.

"Thanks," he said before marching towards the two tents strategically placed away from the fire twenty yards further up the beach. He unzipped the door of the tent on the left and slid inside.

Che-Maria had disappeared to gather more firewood.

"You have a very interesting friend," Martha said to me. "He's very peculiar."

"I know," I said.

"No, you don't."

"I think I know."

Martha shook her head, giving me a knowing grin.

"It's not even that," she said. "Nothing to do with his personality. I see strange things in him, characteristics that weren't in our Angel Manual. I think he is very special. He is marked. His life has a purpose."

"Well, thanks a lot!" I exclaimed.

"No, no, no," she said. "Not like that at all. It is something much deeper, much vaguer. Something I don't know what."

I paused to let her continue, but she just sat in silence, staring across the lake as the sky began to turn greyer and redder, until a scorching sunset, more spectacular than I had ever seen stretched across the horizon.

CHAPTER 4

The next morning, Robert rose at six, as he did every morning on his way to work at the Post Office, and like the super-manager he yearned to be decided we should all go for a sunrise jog.

He shook the dew off our tent and hollered, "Hey, lovebirds, get up. Time to shake those limbs."

Martha told him to shove off.

Che-Maria was already up, whistling an old Disney song and rattling the pots and pans. I just groaned.

It was inevitable that Martha and I were going to share a tent. We were, after all, posing as a couple. But that Martha and I were not "lovebirds" was understood, if only by the two of us.

The night before, Martha had curled up in the corner of the tent in the tattered sleeping bag I had unburied from my basement, and I had sprawled across the centre of the tent under Robert's camping blanket. It had been a warm night, typical of California in mid-July, and I had rocked myself to sleep, tossing and turning in the sandy darkness. At one point I kicked Martha in my stupor. She rolled over, raised herself up on one elbow, and looked at me with concern.

"Maybe we can use this opportunity to discuss your insomnia," she said.

She just nudged over and kissed me on the forehead.

"But not now," she yawned, and fell back into her pillow.

I rolled over and began counting the number of mosquitoes that buzzed past my ears.

Robert splashed into the lake screaming for us to join him, the jog evidently put off until after breakfast. Martha rested herself on her elbow again and fixed me a stare.

"How did you sleep?" she asked.

"Fitfully," I said.

"Maybe you need a psychiatrist," she joked.

"But I have an angel."

"You're so sweet." She laughed, rubbed her eyes, and sat up cross-legged, straightening the sweatshirt she had slept in. It hung loosely on her supermodel frame, suggesting all the right curves and bumps. She brushed her hair back with her hands, pulling it behind her head, tying it with an elastic.

She yawned.

"Yes, I am an angel," she said. "But I'm no longer a professional. Pull yourself up, there. Let's go for a swim."

But before I could reach for my bathing suit, there was a terrified scream from somewhere out on the beach.

"They've found us! They've found us! They've found us!" Robert yelled, and Martha, suddenly frantic, jumped over me and darted out the door.

I peeked out and saw another van twisting through the trees towards our camping spot. Robert was making a great effort to get to shore, splashing and spraying water everywhere. Martha crouched behind Robert's van, and peered out. Out of the corner of my eye I saw Che-Maria dart into the woods.

Once he reached the beach, Robert rushed to his tent, emerging moments later with a shotgun. By this point, the other van was clearly in sight and heading towards us. It was an old model Volkswagen, brightly painted in pastel colours with flowers and hearts. False alarm, I thought. It's only hippies. Martha should enjoy this.

Six people piled out of the VW after it pulled up parallel to the van already on the beach. Martha was right there to greet them, sensing that these were not only safe people but also ultimately cool. She invited them to the campfire and was pouring them coffee by the time I pulled myself through the tent door.

Robert was still frozen in front of his tent, wielding his shotgun and daring anyone to grab him. When I waved to him that everything was alright, he ignored me and stood his ground.

"It's your life," he said, mumbling through his teeth.

I started towards them. Martha may have jived to the hippies' groove, but I had a different opinion. My experiment with bohemia ended with Pique. That relationship had turned me off gambling with my karma, being true to my birth sign, rummaging through the drawers of my past lives, and generally using every trick in the book to escape from reality.

I knew reality was depressing. I knew the system was stacked against you. Why would I want to remind myself all the time by pretending these things didn't exist? I much preferred staring them in the face, daring them to blink. I knew also this was a paradox, that it was probably a lot more fun to react joyously to life and rollick in the pleasure of the moment the moment it struck you to rollick in the pleasure. I knew this was a sort of meaning, but I couldn't drag myself away from the fact that life was made up of more than just fragmented moments and instants.

Life was a story, a continuum. And stories had deep-rooted meanings — meanings that transcended time and space. This is the type of meaning Martha had been sent to uphold: the cosmic continuum. The history of the universe. The I-don't-know-what-but-I'm-pretty-sure-it-exists ultimate purpose for everything.

"Jon, Jon," a voice called out from behind me. It was Che-Maria. "Is it alright? Is everything OK?"

I turned around, but couldn't see anyone.

"Sure. C'mon out. Everything's fine. It's just a group of hippies."

"Oh, hippies," said a bush. "Then that's good."

Che-Maria appeared from the underbrush, and we walked towards the campfire. Martha was having an animated conversation with a long-haired, bearded man wearing only a leather vest and polka dot boxers. This was Yossarian, the leader. He appeared to be in his mid-forties, but his skin was tanned and tight. From his build, you could have easily mistaken him to be in his twenties, but the greying hair and the slightly sagging wrinkles under his eyes gave him away. He was gesticulating wildly and jumping up and down, talking emphatically. Martha smiled and flirted with him, throwing her head and shoulders back with laughter as his gestures became more exaggerated.

When Che-Maria and I reached the campfire, Yossarian stopped gesticulating and introduced the other members of his gang: Sid, a sallow-looking punk with short, spiky ink-black hair and a dog chain secured with a lock around his neck; Yvette, a frilly blonde woman in a flowing summer dress covered with vines, snakes, and apples; Morrison, a large youth with long, gnarly hair and the beginnings of a beard; Joni, a short, perky red-head who said she was from Saskatchewan; and Ringo, a short, stumpy man with a large nose who stared off across the lake the whole time and took no notice of us.

Che-Maria shook all of their hands, welcoming all of them to share our beach, but she passed on greeting Ringo, giving him a surly look instead. I nodded to each in turn.

"This is Jon and Che-Maria," Martha said.

"Greetings," Yossarian boomed. "Who's the dude with the gun? You cats weren't expecting company, were you?"

Paranoid Robert still hadn't moved.

39

"That's Robert," I said. "Don't worry about him. He's just a little jumpy in the mornings. And, no, we weren't."

"Groovy. Really groovy," said Yvette, and then turned and wandered off in the direction of the woods, taking Ringo and Morrison with her.

Sid plunked himself down in the sand beside the fire and began digging a hole with a frying pan he had pulled out of the container which stored all our utensils and cooking gear.

Joni marched off towards Robert.

"That's cool," Yossarian said. "Everyone's doing their own thing. Man, it's so hard to do your own thing when you're cramped up in a van all the time. And it's great to do it with new people. Fantastic, man. Excellent."

Do what? I thought.

The sun was beginning to rise in the sky.

"Yossarian offered to take us to his commune," Martha said, excited. "It's just a short hike through the trees."

I looked back at Robert. Joni was shoving a flower down the barrel of the shotgun, speaking to him in a soft, sing-song voice about how unnecessary violence was for solving conflicts. Robert said he wasn't solving any conflict, only saving his ass. Joni began dancing in place, waving her arms to her own idiosyncratic rhythm.

This was getting more interesting all the time.

"Great," I said.

"Great," said Che-Maria.

"Don't get us into anything stupid," yelled Robert, who was beginning to suspect something was up.

"Great," said Martha, blushing.

Yossarian said: "Cool, dudes. Just let us unpack first." To Sid he added: "C'mon, man. Let's get the gear together."

Sid, who was making some progress on his hole, set down the frying pan and rambled silently over to the van, following

Yossarian and Martha as they continued their conversation about the place of field mice in the Master Plan.

I returned to my tent for my bathing suit. I had decided to go for a swim after all. Robert drifted over to meet me at the tent door, ducked his head, and led me inside.

"I ain't never seen hippies around here before," he said, worried. "They've always stuck pretty much to the coast."

"It's cool," I said.

"I'm thinking something weird is happening," said Robert.

"More than you suspect," I said, running my hand through my hair. "More than *I* suspect."

"Yeah. Sure, man. I know. Life's confusing and all, but this is out of control."

"I think we're going to their commune," I said.

"I hope not," he said.

"I think I'm sure we are," I said, as if nothing could be more dangerous than taking off into the middle of the largest redwood forest left in California with a group of anonymous freaks, when all the while all you wanted was to escape from the Internal Disciplinary Squad of the Federal Postal Service; not to mention the FBI or the cosmic mercenaries he knew nothing about.

Robert peeked out the door, scanning the scene.

"Your girlfriend's hot for that surfer, Jon. You better convince her to stay here."

"It's OK," I said. "She's not my girlfriend."

"No?" he said, turning around. I thought it was time for a little truth.

"She's my therapist," I said, forgetting something important.

"Therapist?" he asked, sharply. "Therapist?"

I nodded.

"I hate therapists," Robert coughed, staring at me like a cat intent on pouncing.

"I know," I said, sorry I had chosen the wrong truth.

Robert went quiet. The air chilled.

"I think," I said. It was suddenly became very hot in the tent.

"You think what?" Robert demanded.

"I think I know you hate therapists," I explained.

"Of course you know," he said.

"Not really," I said.

"But, yes," he said, forcefully. "You do. I've told you."

"Oh, right," I said, sitting down and crossing my legs. I dropped my head into my hands. Did I know that? Yes. Did I think I knew that? Yes. Did I think I thought I knew that? You bet. Did I think I thought I thought I thought I knew that? Ugh. I was starting to see the weakness of this line of thinking.

I knew Robert hated therapists. He told me never to bring them up in conversation. I looked at him. He seemed too stunned to do anything violent. His mother had had a therapist who'd told her she was suffering from some grievous psychological complex because she had drifted through her life until her sixtieth birthday without once questioning what the people who controlled her life had told her. The therapist advised Robert's mother to go on an extended vacation and find herself before it was too late. That was the last Robert had seen or heard from his mother, with the exception of a number of Christmas cards which had come for a couple of years after she left, but stopped arriving two years ago.

Therapists, therefore, were Robert's least favourite people and a topic to be avoided. I looked up at him and shrugged.

"But it's alright," he said. "Martha's alright."

Then an engine started and Che-Maria appeared at the doorway.

"They're taking Martha away!" she said, hysterical. "They're taking Martha away!"

CHAPTER 5

"Nuts!" Robert shouted, pushing past Che-Maria, shotgun in hand.

"Hey!" Che-Maria stumbled after him, warning him to watch for the Frisbee darts. I followed them both, though I sensed my participation in the event was going to be limited — as usual — to a passive acceptance of the consequences.

Out on the beach, I picked up a rock to hurl after the retreating van, but before I could turn my body to throw it, Robert unloaded the gun on them, so I just as quickly dropped it. It wasn't that I didn't know how to act. When I was a kid, I used to get into street fights at the slightest provocation, like someone calling my dad a Republican, or saying my mother slept with Madonna. "Who hasn't?" I would yell at my teasers before bloodying their faces. I was quite a terror, actually. It wasn't until I reached my middle teen years that I mellowed out and became obsessively introverted. One day I suddenly realized I wasn't acting, only re-acting. I was fighting *against* things, but never *for* anything. This didn't seem like such a good idea to me. Logically extended, there would eventually be nothing left. So I tried to think of positive, creative, and constructive changes I could make. I wanted to help build the New World Order George Bush had promised so long ago, but which had somehow never materialized. Like Roosevelt's New Deal, the New World Order had a habit of falling apart.

The van was already in the trees when Robert's blast shook the beach, starting the frogs off on a horrendous croaking spree and shaking a horde of birds out of the trees. He missed his target. The van continued to bounce out of sight.

That first night back at my place in Venice Beach, Martha and I had discussed the possibility of such an event as this. She never wanted to leave me, she had said. She wanted us to be together forever. In fact, one day she wanted to marry me — one day — when I had finally resolved all my problems and she had landed a new occupation. If we ever did get separated — we had promised back in my bedroom — we would devote our full existence to search for the other.

Martha, of course, had the supreme advantage in such an eventuality, with all her angel powers of perception and control over time and space. If she disappeared, there wasn't much I could do, except cross my fingers and pretend to pray. There wasn't anyone in Heaven to pray to, anyway. At least there wasn't anyone there who would be sympathetic enough to help a runaway angel.

Robert pointed towards the van, and we all rushed towards it. "Get in! Get in!" Robert jumped into the driver's seat and started the engine. It roared for a second, then died.

"Nuts!" he yelled. "My van's been sabotaged!"

He tried again, without luck. I stood in the sand beside Che-Maria, staring with her into the trees that had swallowed the kidnappers. She picked up Sid's frying pan, which was lying nearby, and hurled it towards the void that had taken Martha. It landed with a thud twenty yards beyond us.

She turned to me, crying, and I held her. Robert sat slouched in the driver's seat, banging his head lightly against the steering wheel.

"Jon," said Che-Maria. "This is not good."

"No," I said.

"We must do something."

"Yes."

Robert stepped out of the van and began pacing back and forth on the beach with long, heavy strides.

Che-Maria and I followed.

"We must pray," said Che-Maria.

I said: "I think not."

The wind picked up and a sandstorm engulfed us. We moved around the other side of the van to get away from the blowing sand, and I saw then, lying on the beach half-buried, Martha's beautiful torn and tattered patched Bag of Miracles.

What a stroke of luck! Whoever it was that had taken Martha had left us with the best possible device for tracking her down, if only we could figure out how to use it.

Whenever I was with Martha and we found ourselves in a sticky situation, all she had to do was reach into the Bag and the answer produced itself.

I picked up the bag, slung it over my shoulder, and reached inside. It contained an envelope, addressed "To whom it may concern". I showed it to Robert, who immediately ripped it open.

Dear Friend,

Fate has spun its untimely web, and we are all but caught in its trap unless we are quick and wily enough to dart and evade it.

By the time this letter reaches you, however, it may already be too late. You must act as if it is not. There are strange stirrings afoot in the land, and we must all learn to play our parts.

Peace and harmony are in jeopardy. Evil and discord have grown to set foot where they have never been before. Only the actions of friends are to be trusted. Appearances in these trying times are easily deceptive. Beware!

The act you must perform, and you must do this with great haste, taking every precaution because the performing of it will be anticipated by our enemies, is to meet with our regional agent at the Royal Oaks Inn in Pipsquin, California, between the hours of 1:00 p.m. and 2:00 p.m. any weekday ASAP.

He will know you. Come alone.

For the freedom of the universe, be strong!

Sincerely,
(signed) Your Pal

Robert looked up from the letter and stared at me.
"Say what?" he puzzled.
All the time I had known Martha, I had never known the handbag to contain a letter, but apparently one of its functions was to act as a sort of cosmic fax machine, transporting cosmic directives about the universe. All the times I had seen Martha use her magical sack, devices had emerged from it, devices that could be used right at the moment of crisis, like that used copy of *The Second Sex*.

There wasn't much the letter could do to help us get Martha back. It offered no magic spell we could cast to reverse time or pull back the hippies. I took the letter from Robert and read it over. The letter, surely, was meant for Martha, but what did it mean? "Fate has spun its untimely web." That's obvious, I thought: chaos reigns supreme. But "Your Pal"? Huh?

The letter lacked the formality of the memo to Martha from the Supreme Cosmic Command I had read earlier in the week. That communiqué was formal, professional, and cool; this was warm, personal, and, well, mystic, like something out of J.R.R. Tolkein. It had a Middle-Earth quality, and a certain magic.

Then I knew. I got it. I felt at that moment what Robert must have felt when he had picked up that piece of paper in the Special Services mail room — scared and exhilarated. But whereas Robert couldn't see any meaning behind his action, for me patterns were beginning to emerge. Events were beginning to fall into place. Pieces of previously discontinuous information were stringing themselves together, haunting me, pushing me to new limits of understanding. I was certain that before things were over we would be given a full explanation, that Martha was right — life did have meaning — but we would have to hold up our end of the bargain, plug ourselves into the system and connect with whomever this person was that Martha was supposed to meet.

Robert had said he had picked up the message and hadn't understood why, but there hadn't been a reason in any sense Robert would have understood. The reason was in the action; simply acting had been reason enough. By acting, Robert had shaken off his lethargy and produced, through a disruption within his normally unconscious-subconscious self, meaning, a relation of events — the event as it happened, his picking up of the message, and the event as he thought it ought to have happened. He had created an ethical crisis, probably the first in his life, and he had stood up on the side he perceived as truth and justice. Voila! Meaning!

Reading the letter, I experienced a similar disruption. My first reaction was to ignore it, pass it on to someone else, but there was no one else to pass it on to. Neither Robert nor Che-Maria could be expected to deal with the complexity of a cosmic disorganization they knew nothing about, and Martha was gone. The future of the universe rests with me, I thought. No time for thinking about thinking. There was only time for action.

I folded the letter and put it back in its envelope. It didn't seem the time or place right then to let Robert and Che-Maria in on the secret of Martha being an angel and all, though I knew the moment was fast approaching. "The freedom of the universe" would need everyone's co-operation, and, after all, Martha had said Robert was special. I was sorry Martha hadn't said the same of Che-Maria, but Martha's angel perception couldn't have been working at peak capacity if she didn't see she was about to be kidnapped by a group of wandering hippies. Maybe Che-Maria would play an even bigger part than Robert. It seemed likely. She was far more spiritual. I was sure to have a part to play as well, and I was beginning to see what it might be. I was beginning to understand I couldn't always wait for an answer before acting. I was beginning to believe in spontaneity. And I knew these things. I didn't think I knew them!

"Get in the van," I said. "Where's Pipsquin?"

"Just down the road," Robert answered. "But — "

"Just get in," I said. "We have miles to go before we sleep."

And when I leapt into the van and turned the key, the engine instantly roared to life. Robert and Che-Maria jumped in. I pointed the van through the trees, smashed it through the underbrush. Robert and Che-Maria gripped each other as the bumps bounced them about in the passenger seat beside me, Robert reading the letter again, fumbling to understand. He kept opening and closing his mouth, searching for a question, but he knew nothing and, therefore, had no place to begin.

"I still don't get it," he said, finally.

"Which part?" I asked, turning out onto the highway, the sun burning in our faces.

"All of it."

Che-Maria asked, "What does this have to do with Martha?"

"Everything," I said, and then I started at the beginning and told them the whole story, finishing with us in the van just as we drove into Pipsquin's town limits, right in the middle of rush hour and the town's annual homecoming parade.

CHAPTER 6

In the beginning, I said (and most of what follows I learned from Martha), were the Heavens and the Earth. The Heavens were perfectly ordered and the Earth was perfectly chaotic. Everything in Heaven made sense, and nothing on Earth made sense. No third place called "Hell" existed. God ruled Heaven and nobody ruled Earth. Earth was, after all, perfectly chaotic.

One day God decided he wanted to turn Earth into an ordered place, too, but because God had no experience with chaos, only order, the task proved to be more difficult than he had originally anticipated. This is why, in fact, Earth is still not an ordered place today. God has yet to understand the relationships of chaotic functions. There's even a rumour that God has a problem with certain aspects of high school calculus, and anything related to relativity is just beyond him. For God, either things are or they aren't.

Anyway, one day God called together the angels of his inner-court and told them what he was planning:

God: Now that I've got you all together, I want you to know I've been thinking about that blue marble out in space many of you have been referring to as "Earth". I know many of you are anxious to colonize the planet; some of you have even taken more than a passing interest in the creatures that call that place home, particularly the ones you call "people". But before we do anything, we need a plan.

And then God told the angels of his inner-court his idea to create order out of chaos and bring meaning to the planet Earth:

God: We're going to write a book, and this book will contain the Word of God, but first we must give the creatures language so that they may understand the meaning of the book. Only then will order emerge out of chaos. I need a volunteer to go to the planet Earth and give people language.

Lucifer: I will go.

God: Excellent, Lucifer. I knew it would be you. You must go at once and show people their tongues and the names of things. You must begin to show them that existence is meant to be codified and ordered.

Lucifer: Yes. I will go at once.

And so Lucifer went and began to talk to people and tell them the names of things. The first person he met was Atom. That's what Lucifer named him, anyway, since this person had no language, and thus no name:

Lucifer: You are Atom.

Atom: (?)

Lucifer: This is an apple. On your tongue is a thing called language. Can you say *apple?*

Atom: Apple. (Enter Eve)

Lucifer: Who's this?

Atom: Apple.

Lucifer: No (pointing to apple), this is an apple.

Atom: Apple, apple, apple.

Eve: Apple, apple.

Lucifer: No, no. Forget about the apple. (To Eve) You are Eve.

Atom: Eve, Eve.

Eve: Apple, apple.

Lucifer: No, Eve. Forget about the apple.

Atom: Apple, apple, apple.

Lucifer: Eve, this is Atom.

Eve: Atom, Atom, apple.

Lucifer: No. Forget about the apple.

Atom: Apple.

Lucifer: Forget about the apple! In fact, if you go near an apple again, you're going to regret it. Understand?

Eve: Eve.

Atom: Atom.

Lucifer: Good. Now leave me alone and go play in the trees.

Back in Heaven, God recorded the whole scene for his book. He wanted to record everything for posterity. He also wanted to use the book to show people how bad things had been before he had brought them order. But as God observed Lucifer's initial contact with people, he was saddened to realize even he couldn't make sense of the encounter. People made no sense at all. They were totally absurd. What was all that chatter about? Why hadn't Adam and Eve (for God had misheard Lucifer's first label) answered simple questions? What was that business with the apple? God filled in the blanks as best he could before passing off his writing task to the Holy Ghost. Meanwhile, Lucifer was busy handing over the Ten Commandments to Moses, well on his way to setting up a codified society —

"Wait a minute," said Robert. "Lucifer gave Moses the Ten Commandments? I thought he was the bad guy."

"Not yet," I said.

"But what about Job, Abraham and Sarah, Noah? What about all those people? Wasn't Lucifer messed up with them, too?"

"Oh, sure," I said. "But he was still God's agent, then. He only became the bad guy after he and God had a falling out."

"Over what?" asked Che-Maria.

"I'm coming to that," I said, and went on with my story, telling them how just before Christ's appearance on Earth, Lucifer had all but given up hope of achieving his mission, so God recalled him to Heaven for a vacation:

Lucifer: It's hopeless. They'll never learn. They keep changing their minds all the time, making up new meanings for everything even after I explained and explained and explained that order means holding things together, restricting things, making sure everything always stays the same. The more I show them order, the more they cling to chaos!

Thus Lucifer was the first angel to know defeat, and God decided to replace him with Jesus, God's one and only son (God being a single parent). Lucifer sulked around Heaven for a couple of days until God could no longer stand his imperfect behavior and threw him out of the Cosmic City. So Lucifer left, and since he didn't want to return to Earth, he decided to raise Hell. Once there, though, he grew lonely and began to think of returning to Earth to complete his original mission. By this time, however, Jesus, who had gone to Earth in the guise of a man — not an angel — was approaching the time when he would begin his ministry. Lucifer confronted him in the desert:

Jesus: Have you come to tempt me?

Lucifer: No, man. I've come to talk.

Jesus: About what?

Lucifer: About this business of turning Earth into an ordered place. I've come to tell you it's impossible.

Jesus: Go away.

Lucifer: I'm telling you, man, it's fruitless. This place will never be ordered. What you've got to get people to understand is that there's only so much they can do. Earth is a chaotic place, and if people cling to order, they will only be destroyed. You have to teach them to be flexible.

Jesus: I will teach them that order is the only way.

Lucifer: Teach them to come together, right now —

Jesus: Over me?

Lucifer: Sure. Over anything. Just teach them to respect each other; that's the best you'll be able to do.

Then Lucifer went back to Hell, where he began collecting the souls of people who fell short of God's Heaven-o-Meter, a scale set up by Gabriel to measure the eternal worthiness of souls.

Meanwhile, Jesus went about his mission, meeting with mixed success. He told people their lives needed order, and he told them to respect each other, too. He thought it best to hedge his bets. He was beginning to get hip to what Lucifer had said to him. Originally he had thought that once people saw Truth — the value of order — they would line up behind him. But this didn't happen. Some people did line up, but they were all men, and numbered only twelve. Some of them even had to be coerced with promises they would experience real order — Heavenly Order — once they died. Death was real important to people, Jesus found, and he comforted them as best he could with stories about his childhood, about Heaven, about the bliss he thought they would want to achieve on Earth. But while people were pleased things would get better after they died, for the most part they were more interested in living their lives than in creating order. And the process of living had a nasty habit of creating more and more chaos. It was all very counter-productive. Like Lucifer before him, Jesus experienced the frustration of *almost* communicating his message before watching it fracture into smaller and smaller divergent bits — bits that would never come together again, bits that could be twisted to mean things he never intended them to mean.

Then one day, the Earthly authorities with a vested interest in chaos decided Jesus' ministry was infringing on their ability to manipulate people. Ironically, the authorities that eventually killed Jesus were the ones set up by Lucifer hundreds of years earlier to achieve the same goal — a unified social order — that Jesus had been sent to Earth to secure:

God: You're back! Have you brought order to Earth?

Jesus: No, much worse. I fear I have only more deeply entrenched chaos in an already fragile ecosystem.

God: What happened?

Jesus: They killed me.

God: Why?

Jesus: Apparently, I irritated them.

God: This is no good. You must go back. I will have the Holy Ghost provide you with a revised schedule of goals and procedures. (To Gabriel, who was hovering nearby) Fetch the Holy Ghost, Gabby. I'm convening an emergency session of the Cosmic Council.

It was at that council meeting that God finally relented to the opinion that order would likely never come to Earth, though it was the duty of all under his command to keep trying. God declared, therefore, that in the immediate present, which was two thousand years ago now, the best that could be hoped for on Earth was the appearance of order. Order would be presented to people in the form of knowledge, free will, religion, other humanistic studies and arts — all of which were already thriving on the planet, and all of which had originally been set up by Lucifer as part of his compromise solution to the Divine Plan:

God: From the intelligence we've gathered, you can see that a semblance of order exists on Earth. What's left to do now is the creation of the belief that the appearance is the reality. The Holy Ghost has drafted a plan that will ensure that out of this illusion, over which the powers of Heaven will have ultimate control, order will eventually emerge. I have sent Jesus back to Earth to begin the first phase of this plan.

Thus, I said, the creation of the biblical myth as we have come to know it began. God sent Jesus back to Earth to proclaim his divine origin and begin the process of Heavenly Order on Earth.

I paused and looked over at Robert and Che-Maria, only to see the two of them entranced in the story. The road was a blur. I was excited. Everything was making sense.

"What's this to do with Martha?" blurted Robert. "I mean, so what? Order, chaos, order, chaos. We have a real problem here."

I waved him off.

"Do you remember the fuss about that Madonna concert a few years ago?" I said.

"Sure."

"And do you remember the hullabaloo in the press about the break in the cosmic membrane?"

"Yeah."

"Well, Martha is one of them. An angel. She came to Earth as part of God's plan to stimulate order, to finally bring about the culmination of the Holy Ghost's plan."

"I thought she was different," said Che-Maria.

"Yeah," said Robert. "I knew there had to be more to her than her looks."

"But God's dead," I said. "At least those were the reports Martha was getting. God died around the time of the reformation. That's what all that trouble was about."

Then I told them about my revelation on the beach.

"The reason I called you guys," I said, "was because Martha decided to quit the Angel Corps. She was disillusioned about the death of God and stuff like that. The cosmic command was beginning to institute a cosmic re-organization, and she had bad feelings about it."

Robert and Che-Maria stared at me in silence.

"We called you guys so we could get away, but obviously the powers-that-be were stronger than we thought. They snatched Martha away. The letter, I think, was an attempt to warn her. I think the reference to the meeting in Pipsquin is essential to the well-being of the universe. The cosmos depends on us," I said.

Pipsquin's homecoming parade ground traffic to a halt, and we sat stalled in our van as sixteen-year-old marionettes paraded before us twirling their batons, a brass band marching in step behind them.

The future of the universe, I thought. Wow.

CHAPTER 7

The Royal Oaks Inn was a fake Elizabethan pub with artificial thatch and a plastic door-knocker. It faced directly onto the parade route. Above the door, a brightly-coloured sign proclaiming the best draught in the state swung lightly in the breeze.

Parade watchers crowded the entrance. We had to squeeze past the crowd into the pub's hallway, then into the pub itself. The ceiling, separated by expansive parallel cross-beams, hung low, barely over our heads. Che-Maria watched the parade out of the window. Robert moved to the bar and ordered two beers.

"The letter said 1:00 or 2:00, hey Jon?" he asked.

"Yeah."

"What time is it?"

"12:30."

I hadn't bothered to tell Robert and Che-Maria some of Martha's bigger secrets, like how the Bible was revised by the Holy Ghost to paint Lucifer as the Evil One. The idea had been to convince people that meaning was formed in opposition. For example, day is defined against night, male against female, politicians against Sunday School teachers. Each half of the pair represented a thing, an entity, a meaning. The revised Bible painted Lucifer as the source of Earth's chaos, even though everyone in Heaven knew chaos had been there all along. People were beginning to figure that out, too. At the end of the last century people were beginning to understand that meaning was produced in the space between the binary, and not in either of the binary's elements.

Like I said earlier, that's why the angels first began appearing on Earth: to straighten out the mess and restore order to meaning.

Another of Martha's secrets was the Holy Ghost's and Gabriel's plan to disguise Richard Nixon as the Second Coming. When that failed, they manipulated the karma of Ronald Reagan, a plan which had considerably more luck, even though Rompin' Ronnie failed to trigger the nuclear Armageddon they had hoped would blow the Earth out of existence altogether.

Che-Maria motioned for me to come join her by the window.

"Look at that man across the street, Jon," she said. "Do you recognize him?"

The man was tall with long hair. He wore mirrored sunglasses, a white T-shirt, and khaki shorts. It only took me a second.

"That's Yossarian," I said, stunned.

"I thought so," said Che-Maria. "We must be careful."

She waved to Robert, who had engrossed himself in the Jays-Angels game. He left the game grudgingly, pulling himself slowly from his bar stool to join us at the window.

"Yossarian is on the street," Che-Maria said. "Look."

Robert gave two quick shoulder checks, scanning the pub.

"Nuts!" he said. "That letter's probably a trap. We gotta split." He shoved me towards the door as he grabbed Che-Maria's hand and began to lead us back onto the street, but Che-Maria pulled us back.

"Upstairs," she said, pointing towards a stairway at the back of the room. "Go upstairs and wait for me."

I took three steps towards the stairs before I realized Robert had not followed. He had stopped to argue with her. I reached out, grabbed him by the arm, and pulled him up the stairs with me.

The stairs led to a hallway, and the hallway led to a platform that overlooked the street. I could see Yossarian hiding behind his sunglasses, whispering every couple minutes into a walkie-talkie. Robert leaned over the railing, grumbling. He glanced up and down the parade route before quickly jumping back and staring at me.

"They're all here," he said. "All those hippie dips. They're all over the place. We've been banished to Hippie Hell!"

Looking over the railing, I saw what he said was true. There was Sid and Morrison, Yvette and Joni, Ringo and Yossarian. They were all here, spread strategically up and down the parade route at twenty yard intervals, each with a walkie-talkie and sunglasses, the people of Pipsquin surrounding them, encompassing them, oblivious to their imminent danger. I looked about for Martha, but I couldn't see her.

Che-Maria appeared behind us. She had a man with her. She was holding his hand, pulling him into the sunlight on the balcony. He was wearing a trench coat over a three-piece suit. He had short, slick hair, and his mouth held the chomped butt of a cigar.

"Robert, Jon, I want to introduce a friend," she said.

Robert stared at the man suspiciously. Che-Maria turned slowly from her husband to me. I reached out my hand.

"Hi," I said. "I'm Jon."

The man nodded. Robert finally introduced himself.

"Nasty scar on your hand there," he said. "How did you manage that?"

"Cut myself shaving," the man said, smiling.

"Seriously?" Robert asked, before Che-Maria spanked him.

"Don't you know who this is?" she asked.

"No."

"This is Jesus Christ."

"Oh," said Robert, turning to face the Prince of Peace, blushing. "Sorry to hear about your dad."

Jesus smiled at him. "He's not dead," he said.

"No?"

"No."

"Oh," said Robert. "Well, that's good then."

I glanced across the street to see if Yossarian was still in his place. He wasn't.

"We better split," I said, starting towards the door. "The hippies are on the move."

"No, that's OK," Jesus said. "They work for me."

"For you?"

"Yes."

"Well, what about Martha?" Robert asked.

"In good time, my friend," Jesus said, waving him off. "First, we need to meet up with Lucifer. Come."

We descended back through the door and down the staircase into the bar. Yossarian's band was spread about the room, but they took no notice of us, and we ignored them. Jesus, still holding Che-Maria's hand, led us through a doorway into the kitchen and finally down another set of stairs to the wine cellar — a small, dark, musty, room lined with bottles of fermenting grape juice.

When we were all there, Jesus pulled a cigarette lighter from his pocket and lit the half dozen candles that were spread about the room.

"This doesn't involve any chanting, does it?" Robert asked, blowing into his hands. "Any hocus-pocus?"

"No," said Jesus. "Just sit still. You'll see."

We sat quiet for half-an-hour, waiting. And waiting. I was beginning to think about how drafty the room was when I realized that within this enclosed basement there existed a definite cross-breeze, and it was picking up. The light from the candles bounced violently off the walls.

I looked at Jesus, but his eyes were closed. A figure was materializing in the corner, the way Martha had done in my bedroom closet, but it wasn't her. The wind died down. The figure was complete. Lucifer?

If this is Lucifer, I thought, he needs to hire a public relations firm because people have totally the wrong impression. He looked more like the librarian of my junior high school than the Lord of Darkness, though my experiences with librarians had sometimes led me to suspect them to be of a sinister nature.

Well groomed and young, he smiled broadly at everyone.

"How can I help you, Lord of Hosts?" he addressed Jesus. "I came as soon as I got your Urgent Message. What's up?"

Jesus coughed.

"The Holy Ghost and Gabriel have concocted a plot to take over the universe," he said. "It's a conspiracy that is well along."

"I know," said Lucifer. "I'm well-informed. I have spies."

"As I am aware," said Jesus. "But because you are so well-informed, you also know that I have been away for the past half-century on a fact-finding mission to another dimension. I have only heard of these events recently, and, upon finding of them, I fled the Cosmic City. It now seems that I, too, may be in danger."

"Ah," said Lucifer. "I know not seems. Indeed, you are in danger. And you have come to me for help? How strange."

"Not so," said Jesus. "My present action is far less strange than you imagine, for you see, God is not dead as you think. He is alive and imprisoned. I have come to you so that you may help us free him."

At this point, a puzzled look came across Lucifer's face and he began pacing the room. "Not dead," he said. "Not dead. Could my intelligence be so misinformed?"

"I swear to you Lucifer, it is true," said Jesus. "He has been imprisoned for three hundred years. At first, he announced he was going on sabbatical for a couple of centuries. This is where I thought he was when I left on my journey. This is where he is supposed to have died. Now I realize the whole event has been staged; that everything resulted from the will of the Holy Ghost and Gabriel to dominate. They want to create a new order and place themselves at the head of it."

"Sacred Blood!" exclaimed Lucifer. "If God's still alive, then there's hope yet!"

"My thoughts exactly," said Jesus. The two men stared at each other and nodded some tacit agreement.

I wanted to ask about Martha, but the conversation between the two deities had left me terribly confused. Not so Robert.

"Hey!" he said. "What gives? What about Martha? What about us?"

This outburst startled Jesus, who had apparently forgotten we were there. He smacked his forehead, reached into the pocket of his overcoat, and pulled out a piece of paper which he handed to me.

Dear Jon,

My Lord has come for me, and I must follow. He has assured me you will be taken care of. You must trust him. I have another mission which takes me away from you. The matter is grave and the business urgent. Still, I have not forgotten you and hope to see you soon.

I meant to tell you before I left that you are only as ill as you perceive yourself to be. The power to control your destiny is within. You must take hold of this power and use it to your advantage.

If you have received this letter, you are well on the way to that realization yourself. You're a special person, Jon. I love you.

(signed) Martha XXX

Attached to the letter was this poem.

decentred love

I still want to hold your hand
make love to/with you on an empty beach
watch you slowly undress and step
into a bubblebath and
I want you to want these things too
to speak what you feel with what you feel
is your voice I will listen
do not be afraid of my/our love and fecundal religion

"I forget where I first heard this," Martha had written underneath, "but it has always stuck with me."

I folded the letter and put it in my pocket. Jesus glanced about the room.

"We have little time," he said. "We must go to Heaven immediately."

Lucifer nodded. There was a flash of light, and we were there.

CHAPTER 8

How to describe Heaven? Everyone wants to know. It's the first thing people ask me after they find out about my adventures. What's it like? Usually I tell them that the first thing I thought of after being transported to Eternity was the Emerald City in *The Wizard of Oz*.

I don't mean that the Cosmic Forces are like the façade of a wizard pulling levers behind a curtain. No. Everything in Heaven is real. Real as real. Real as the blood in your veins. People may not want to believe that, and that's okay with me. I didn't quite believe it myself until the smoke cleared and we found ourselves standing outside of a building that looked a little like Buckingham Palace. Sometimes your expectations are met, and sometimes they're exceeded. Sometimes reality falls short. Heaven was strange because it didn't do any of these things. It just was. It was there, and you were there, and it was all around you, and you felt warm and comfortable, like you were at home on your couch watching a hockey game and the home team was winning but you didn't really care.

After we arrived things happened pretty fast. A lot of what I saw I'm not allowed to tell you, and what I didn't see I haven't learned too much about.

You can be sure, though, that Martha was at the heart of it. After she disappeared on the beach, the hippies took her to Pipsquin to meet Jesus. Then she led the negotiations to secure the Supra-Cosmic Summit between the Prince of Peace and the Prince of Darkness. Because she was a fallen angel, Martha had credibility in the eyes of Lucifer's agents. She, too, had broken ranks with the ideology of Heaven. She, too, had rebelled against the dominant order and had chosen to live on the margin. When Jesus called her to Pipsquin she was an angel at risk of losing her identity. She saw that Heaven had been manipulated and fragmented, and had thus jumped into an Earthly frame. She had gone on the road, the endless highway, where all answers are over the horizon. Martha told me later that if she had lived the life of the road, that would have killed her, too. Life needed structure, not just moving on, moving on. The Holy Ghost and Gabriel wanted too much structure, but they weren't completely wrong. Martha didn't belong in a tent; she was capable of so much more.

As for me, right now I'm back in California sitting straight up in bed, my laptop on my knees, my imagination in the stars. How's that, eh? I threw that cliché in for you literary types, to give you something to complain about. *The Cosmic Press* keeps sending me offers to tell my story, but I'm in no hurry. *The New York Times* says if my news is fit to print, they'll take it when I'm ready. Robert says my scribblings have the potential to be a bestseller, but I don't care about the money. I just want to be left alone.

Martha still comes to visit once and a while, even though she's not allowed. Next summer, she's going to ask for a vacation. We're planning on renting a car and driving to New York City, like we meant to do before the future of the universe got in the way. Sometimes we go for walks along the beach, but nobody asks her to expose herself anymore. Nobody even stares at her, though I think she's more beautiful than ever.

Earth has become a more peaceful place. People have learned to respect each other. Martha's still got her Bag of

Miracles, and it's a little more worn and a little more torn. It gets more practical with age. That's what I was thinking about after the first time we made love — how things get more practical with age. The dressing falls off. Either people are less inclined to believe in illusions or they're more able to see stories for what they are. Nursery rhymes, fairy tales, and myths. One way, the other, or both — the wise mature beyond the sensation and start digging deeper for the experience.

When you really want to understand something, anything that hinders your quest — like the frivolous mind-games of youth — is frustrating and disheartening, and you want to be rid of it. My point here is that the Earth has really only been exposed to language for a short period of time — we're so bloody young, yet — and we are only starting to understand what it means to be alive.

The only thing that puzzles me is Martha's comment about the special nature of Robert's soul. Martha's comment had seemed significant, but nothing ever became of it. When I asked her about it yesterday, she promised to fax me a response. "Let me think about it," she said. The fax came while I was banging out Chapter Three, and I have been saving it all this time.

> Dear Jon,
>
> I was speaking with Hemingway yesterday. He advised me to tell you to forget your personal tragedies. Carpe Diem, Jon. Seize the day.
>
> As for your question about Robert, I honestly can't remember saying that. I checked my files, but they contained nothing pertinent. It probably wasn't important — just an inkling. You know what I mean. Every premonition can't be right.

I hope your book's coming along. I'd love to read it once you're finished. Your mother's doing well. Give my love to your goldfish, especially Caesar.

The negotiations are going well, too. Everything should be ironed out by Friday of next week, and then we can get started on the grievance claims. So many souls are claiming to have been improperly judged, of being sent wrongly to Hell. Billions. And they all want compensation. I'm not sure what we have to give, really.

I hope this has been a help to you. See you soon.

Martha XXX

So there you go. Angels aren't perfect, after all.

Without Contraries is no progression. Attraction and Repulsion, Reason and Energy, Love and Hate, are necessary to Human existence.

☙

The road of excess leads to the palace of wisdom.

— William Blake, *The Marriage of Heaven and Hell*

Gerry

Midnight is long past.

It's late fall. You're on your way home after a night of playing pool with friends. Six months ago, you graduated from university. Now you're walking home, north, away from the subway, through the streets of your childhood, sinking into the shadows.

You nearly walk into him before you see him.

"Hey, brother," you say, staggering to avoid a collision. You note him: the oddity of him, the short steps that carry him forward, his mumbling, and the stubble on his face; his lean body stuffed into a soiled sweater and wrapped in a battered, red leather jacket, ripped under the sleeves.

He says nothing, doesn't even look at you, but shuffles along the street, one boot after the other, keeping a rhythm only he can hear.

The next day, you see him again. Expressionless, he glides past your house, doing that same funeral walk. Your mother says he appeared on your porch last week and asked for a glass of water. His name is Gerry. He lives with his grandmother. His mother died a month ago. Cancer. And he's not a Vietnam vet, which is what you figured. You imagine American cities swarm with people like him, trapped in their jungle nightmares.

"Cindy called again," your mother says.

You're pouring milk over your cereal, struggling to take in the new day. Cindy emerged a month ago to confront you with memories, her body a shining promise, her tales sharpened like pointed sticks. She took you dancing, regaled you with descriptions of California, Texas, mountains, deserts, golden beaches and crazy people, luxurious apartments, renegades, promising artists, and barren wantonness: the nuts and bolts of humanity; the rainbow and the nightmare; the ghouls and the keepers of the light.

"I've changed," she said, but you couldn't see it.

The first girl to love you, the first girl to fuck you, the first girl to open you up, the first girl to break you down, the first girl to run away. She retained her complications, continued to be bound by optimism and fear, hope and death.

Opportunity blooms in crisis, you remind yourself. Wisdom rises out of experience.

You prepare to phone Cindy, collect the debris of your past and move on. You are scaling another mountain. She answers the phone, and you find yourself telling her about Gerry: how he passes your house at least once every other day about the time you finish your first cup of coffee; how you sometimes see him on your way to work, though you're sure he has never seen you.

Border Guard

The car idled. Jerome tucked a cigarette behind his ear. He didn't know if he ought to be there, parked opposite the sports bar where Cynthia worked.

A light snow powdered the hood of his car.

He rubbed his hands together and turned off the engine. Two hours earlier he had come home from work and found a message on his answering machine: "Jerome. Call me."

From his sister. His father was dying.

Jerome slammed shut the door of his Thunderbird. He trudged across the street towards the bar. He was aware Cynthia didn't want to see him — though not why she had cut him off — yet the news of his father's impending death gave him an excuse, he thought, to try one more time. He didn't want to go home alone; would she come with him?

She was twenty-one. So she said. He thought maybe she was eighteen. He was chasing thirty. He started coming to the bar after Dorothea moved out, came early, drank late. Then after twelve drunken nights and hungover days, he sat one more time on the last stool against the wall and watched Cynthia refill drinks.

Finally, she said to him: "You look interesting. What's your name?"

She was wearing a tight top, her hair pulled back. He read her body language: I'm no pushover, no weakling. He told her his name. His job. About his wife.

"What happened?" she asked.

"It's a long story."

"Tell me."

She crossed her hands on the bar, leaned forward on her elbows. Pushed her face toward him.

They met at university. They were friends before they were lovers. He was studying to be a teacher, but dropped out before he finished his degree.

He grew up on a farm, the grandson of Russian immigrants. His parents were deeply religious. After high school he spent a year in town living above a convenience store, working odd jobs, and trying to bed the girl his landlord hired to work at the store on weekends.

"I felt free for the first time in my life," he told Cynthia, "but I had no direction."

He enrolled in university. Two-and-a-half years later he ran off to Prague. Barriers were falling. Commentators proclaimed "the end of history." The Berlin Wall, reduced to fragments, was stuffed into two-inch square boxes and sold to tourists. Everything, anything, seemed possible, and he felt sure he would find his new self in the ruins of the Old World.

"I met this girl. She worked at the hostel where I first stayed. She was wonderful, beautiful, articulate, talented. She seemed to know everything. I was wide open for new experiences, and I fell hard for her. She was like no one I had ever met."

"Who was she?"

"If I knew, I'd tell you."

"What is that supposed to mean?"

"Do you believe in love?" he asked.

"Love at first sight you mean?"

"Total blinding dependency."

She laughed. "Not if you put it like that."

"That's how it was with this girl in Prague. All I knew was I needed her, and I didn't know who she was or why she ought to be so important to me. I didn't know if it was her or if it was me. So when it didn't work out, I fell apart. My insides burned, just raged. I spent seven days in my room and drank sixteen or twenty bottles of wine. Then I came home and married my wife."

"For the safety," Cynthia said.

"Something like that," Jerome agreed.

"You still haven't told me why she left."

So he told her. He told her, and asked for his bill, and she slipped him her phone number.

"Call me," she said. "You tell interesting stories."

Jerome entered the bar. It was early yet. The room was barely half full. He found a table with a view of the door and a view of the bar. He lit his cigarette and tried to imagine the scene at home: his father in the hospital; his sister and her husband; his brother. So it's almost over, he thought. His father had asked for him, his sister had said. The order had been given: *Tell Jerome to come.* The prodigal son. *Come, Jerome. He wants to see you.* I can't. I have nothing to say.

Two weeks earlier his sister had called. They had argued.

He said: "He always needs to be right. I can't breathe in that house."

She said: "He isn't any more righteous than you, Jerome. Think about what it's like to be between you two."

He couldn't. He couldn't bend. He couldn't imagine reconciliation, only recapitulation. He could not — would not — give up his self-respect, his dignity. The conflict itself. He was who he was because he had flown out of that house, and he would not go back. He would not go back across that barrier, that line.

"It isn't possible to say something that is fair to both of you," his sister had said.

He said: "Linda, please. Don't try to guilt me."

But she wasn't. As he sat in the bar, he marvelled at her insight. No one is right. It's not possible to be fair to both sides at once, when both sides refuse to include the other. Both sides own a portion of the truth, what is real.

He thought of Dorothea. They had married young, younger than most. Her family had been happy with the match, his pleased he had chosen a sensible girl. But had he chosen her? Or had she chosen him? It was true she hadn't given up on him when he returned from Prague. She had missed him. She saw, he thought, a chance to tame him. In her eyes he was wild. He saw himself as lost. He could not be tamed, only found. Dorothea had found him, and for a while calmed him, but when the shock of failed love wore off, his restlessness returned and grew.

"I feel like your prey," he told her in their third year of marriage. They owned a house, two cars, a pool table, and a parakeet.

One night he drove around the city until dawn, then parked in the corner of an arena parking lot, watched the sun come up, and fell asleep. They tried counselling. They tried pornography. They talked about children, but Dorothea thought children deserved a stable family and told Jerome she was losing confidence in his ability to provide one.

"Do you still love me?" she asked.

"It's not you," he told her, though increasingly she seemed foreign. He didn't want the house, the cars, the bird.

When she moved out, she said, "I don't understand you anymore." He put her bags in the car and waved as she drove away.

He told Cynthia that Dorothea had left because she wanted "the whole middle class schtick, and that kind of life felt like crap to me." This made sense to Cynthia since she was running from something similar. As he sat at the bar waiting for her, he realized it was the closest thing to a bond they shared — this sense of life being meant for something beyond the world as it had been handed to them. Dorothea, he knew, felt it too, though to her it meant rising above the slings and arrows of everyday sadness, protecting your island of self-constructed perfection. To Jerome it meant finding gold in the dung heap; beauty in the dark tremors of humanity's struggle. It meant celebrating life as it was — life as it could only be.

On his first date with Cynthia — the first time they got together away from the bar — she told him what it meant for her: The New Age. An era governed by the Rule of Love. An era dedicated to the worship of Gaia, our mother, the Earth.

"It's so simple," she said. "Let your Spirit Self become your guide."

"Is that what you do?" he asked.

"Yes."

Ever since she was a child she had been working to align her Spirit Self with the natural world. "Of course, when I was younger, I didn't know that's what I was doing. I just thought that I liked plants, you know. My mother said I had a green thumb, but I always knew there was more to it. So when I was in high school, this girl explained to me how organized religion was responsible for this belief we have, you know, that humanity is here to control the animals, to exploit nature for its personal gain, and how people are killing the planet; how it's suicidal, because if we kill the planet then, like, where will we live, right? And now we have global warming, and the ozone hole, and all that, right, but people still don't get it. They still don't understand. All things are connected, and it starts with your Spirit Self. Getting yourself right with the universe is the first step. You know what I mean?"

Jerome nodded. "I think so, yes."

"I'm serious," she said.

He tried to smile. "I wish I had your conviction."

"Do you believe in God?" she asked.

"Yes," he said, "but not in salvation."

"I believe in salvation," she said, "but not God. Not really."

"You're like my wife," he said. When she asked him what he meant, he paused, not sure what to reveal. "Dorothea believed in heaven without the judgment, and I suppose I believe in judgment, but not heaven. She left because I couldn't make her happy, because I couldn't accept living happily ever after. She thought I was having an affair, but I wasn't, so I was suffering for something I hadn't done. Then I said I didn't see anything wrong with adultery anyway. How can love be love if it's confining?"

On the television over the bar, Steve Yzerman scored, pushing the Red Wings to a 2-1 lead over the Maple Leafs. Jerome ordered a beer and asked for a newspaper. He watched a couple of college students play pool. A Pink Floyd song blared out of the juke box. When he was a child, his father read the newspaper aloud at the dinner table. Jerome remembered his father's clear syllables rising above the clatter of the cutlery: the certainty in his father's pronouncements about the events of the day, the sharp edges of the old man's view of the world, and his mother attempting to draw her children into conversation.

80

His grandparents came to Canada after Lenin's revolution. They were thrown off the land by the Bolsheviks, broken in spirit. When they came to the New World, they withdrew from life, tried to lose themselves in God. An immigrant family develops its own myths, Jerome thought, about themselves, the past, their neighbours, the world at large. His father talked about the generous wheat fields of Russia as if he had been there: "The land was golden until the Communists burned it." His brother found redemption in the cross. Jerome sought something he felt was more important: freedom.

His beer arrived. He skimmed the newspaper. Stock markets were soaring to record levels. Trouble continued in Iraq, Serbia, the Congo. A two-year-old girl had been found wandering the streets of Saskatoon in the middle of a snow storm.

"Hey, buddy."

Jerome looked up. It was one of the college students.

"Want to shoot some stick?"

Jerome folded his newspaper, glanced behind the bar for Cynthia. She wasn't there. Detroit had taken a 3-1 lead.

"Sure," he said, and stood. "Your partner take off?"

"He has an exam tomorrow."

Jerome picked up his beer and followed the student. The table was already set up. Jerome broke. The student won the first game. Jerome won the second. The tie-breaker ended when Jerome sewered with one ball remaining. "Now you owe me a beer," the student laughed. Jerome waved to the waitress for two more. He sat at the student's table with his back towards the bar.

"I shouldn't be here," he said.

"Why not?"

"My father is dying. He's in the hospital. I came to convince my girlfriend — ex-girlfriend, really — to come with me to see him. She works behind the bar. What do you think?"

"She'll come," the student said.

"She won't."

"Why not? It's an emergency. If she doesn't, forget her."

Jerome said: "The thing is, she left me."

"And you want to know why."

"I want her back."

"For a couple of days."

"For a couple of days," Jerome repeated. Their beers arrived.

"You shouldn't be here," the student agreed. "But what the hell? You got a right to ask."

Jerome picked up his glass. "Cheers."

"I don't want you to remember me," Cynthia had said to him once.

"What are you talking about?" They were in bed. Heavy rain pounded on the windows.

"I don't want you talking about me to other people, other women."

"There are no other women."

"Not now. Later."

It was the only hint Jerome could drag out of his memory that she had moved beyond him. He did not promise to forget her, nor did he probe to find out the source of her comment. What anxiety had provoked it? What fear? What suspicion? What history?

She had practically moved in with him after their first night together. She brought her books, her candles, her incense. She filled his refrigerator with soy milk and yogurt, his cupboards with lentils and beans. She threw out his bacon, his hamburgers, his steaks. He had been in no condition to rebuff her influence. She was in ascension.

At sixteen, she had left home and moved to the city with her boyfriend. She took the first job she could find, baby-sitting a neighbour's kids — Timmy and Sabrina, six and eight. The kids watched television when they weren't at school. Toys, clothes, old newspapers, dirty dishes, video cassettes, and self-help books filled every corner of the apartment. Their mother was a waitress at a local steakhouse. Soon after Cynthia started watching the kids, their mother began sleeping over at her boyfriend's.

"When Sabrina asked me to sign a permission note so she could go on a field trip, I knew it was out of control. My boyfriend was angry, because he never saw me. One day I came home and he was gone."

She got a job at a bookstore, then the job at the bar. Jerome never questioned her interest in him until it was gone. The weekend before the last time he spoke to her, he took her to a play. Students at the university were performing Edward Albee's *Who's Afraid of Virginia Woolf?* They sat in the second row to the left of the stage. It was the first time anyone had taken her to a play. Midway through the first act she started crying. Jerome noticed this when she reached over and covered his hand with hers. Two lines of tears streamed down her face. When they got to his car, she bit his ear. "I want to fuck you, fuck you all night," she said. He slipped his thumb inside the back pocket of her jeans. He wanted to believe explanations were unnecessary for them. He wanted to believe they had moved beyond the game.

Jerome looked up. There she was, her hand on the student's shoulder.

"Can I get you boys anything?"

"No, thanks," said the student.

Jerome said: "Cynthia."

"How are you doing, Jerome?"

"I was waiting for you."

"Evidently."

"I need to talk to you."

"There's nothing to talk about."

"My father's dying."

She bit the end of her pen. "I'm sorry to hear that."

"I need to talk to you."

She paused. "Later," she said. "Okay?"

"Okay." She left.

Jerome knew it wasn't much — what Cynthia could do for him — but it was all he wanted. He was glad he came. He closed his eyes and tried to find the dark centre in the vortex of his mind.

Waiting for a Miracle

A line of light rolls along the wall.

Forty-seven.

The line passes across Robbie's poster of Jimmy Page, over the empty fish tank, catches the end of the Les Paul, and starts breaking up when it drifts over the pile of dirty clothes and disappears into the closet.

Forty-eight, Robbie counts.

Forty-nine.

How come I never noticed the cars before?

A yellow light. Air brakes release. A bus.

Robbie twists his head and looks back over his left shoulder at the window.

It's always been there, he thinks.

The lines of light must have been, too.

Turning around, Robbie sits up, crosses his legs, and scans the room for the mickey of rum.

There's the Coke. The glass.

He sticks his hand up under his T-shirt and scratches his chest.

On the counter in the kitchen, he thinks.

He falls backwards onto the floor and closes his eyes. The light passes over him.

Fifty.

Fifty-one.

If Marie were here, he thinks, *there would be possibilities.*

Another line of light rolls along the wall and disappears into the closet.

Robbie stands.

He has one thought — rum.

The stairs. The light switch. Up, up.

Robbie stumbles. Trips over a pile of comics. Throws himself against the stairwell.

He straightens himself.

He strolls through the living room into the kitchen, hitting the light switch with his elbow as he passes through the doorway.

The rum sits on the table.

Beautiful elixir, Robbie thinks, snatching the bottle in his left hand and spinning around.

Reliever of sorrows, friend of the forsaken, desolate, despondent. Giver of fire.

He stumbles back down the stairs, avoiding the stack of comics, and sits again on the floor in the middle of the room.

No lines of light pass along the wall. He fills half a glass with rum, then tops it up with Coke.

No lines of light.

Robbie reaches for a book to throw at the light switch, and hits it on his first attempt.

The rum rolls warm down his throat.

Monica & Pete

Monica closes the magazine and reaches for her coffee. She thinks about the last sentence she read: *The role of literature is to dramatize our anxieties; to provide dramatic content to the tensions which fill our lives.* She is waiting for Pete, her husband, to return with her cigarettes. She is waiting for the right moment to tell him of her infidelity. Perhaps it will never come. Perhaps that would be best.

Outside, a bird goes spastic in the birdbath Monica has recently installed. Monica watches the bird through the window of the solarium. The bird twitches again, filling the air with its spray. Monica and Pete bought this house a year ago, and they are slowly transforming it in alignment with their tastes; Monica in charge of the exterior, Pete in charge of the interior. In recent days this arrangement has been the source of a lingering unpleasantness. First, Pete bought a pair of garden gnomes at a neighbour's garage sale. Second, Pete placed the gnomes underneath the birdbath. Third, Monica deposited the gnomes in the basement — to the left of the furnace, to the right of the recycling bin, on top of a pile of scrap lumber.

They have been married three years. Monica has had three affairs. Brief affairs. Two did not involve actual sex, that is, intercourse; her one concession — however minute — to propriety; on the other hand, there was touching, there was flesh, there was nakedness. The affairs were definitely indiscretions, disruptions of her relationship with Pete. She knows she has torn the fabric of their trust, their love. Does Pete know? This is the question. Does he suspect? If he doesn't know, what is the damage? Who is the victim?

Not her. Not Monica.

One of the men she got naked with was an ex-flame, an artist. He convinced Pete to commission a painting of Monica so he could get her in the sack. It almost worked. His phone rang at the moment Monica was willing to say yes. Then she thought, no, better not. The artist had been kissing her breasts, massaging her thighs. *To bring out your colour. Yes. Yes. That's good. Good.* She buttoned up her shirt while he was on the phone. "That was New York," he said when he got back. "My agent. I need to go. A magazine wants to do a spread."

Monica's second infidelity occurred in the swimwear section at Eaton's downtown. She was looking for a gift for Pete's sister and made a motion to the saleswoman that she could use some help. The saleswoman directed her to the back corner behind a kayak and kissed her. She said, "You have a beautiful face. Can I kiss you?" She stepped towards Monica and Monica accepted her hands on her waist. "I'm looking for something blue," she said. The saleswoman brushed her hand against Monica's breast and said, "I know just the thing."

The next day they met at a hotel for lunch. The saleswoman rented a room. They talked about the weather. Monica talked about her garden. The saleswoman talked about her husband, how tender he was, how sad. They lay close to each other. They held hands. Kissed. Monica allowed the saleswoman to undress her. Touch her. Hold her. When they stepped into the shower, the saleswoman burst into tears. Monica brushed back her hair, wrapped her in a towel, ordered room service, and turned on the TV.

The magazine Monica is reading was given to her by her most recent lover, a writer. He is an old friend of Pete's. The magazine contains a story by the writer. His name is Darrell. The story is about Darrell as a boy. It is about Darrell's alcoholic father, his promiscuous sister, and Darrell's frantic masturbation habit. Monica supposes the story is not really about any of those things. The essay she has been reading suggests this: *Television teaches people everything important happens on the surface. In previous centuries, educated audiences understood this type of (non-)engagement with narrative to be superficial, over-simplistic. Shakespeare, for example, was entertainment, yes, but it was also a leaping point for larger discussions.* Monica wonders if this is true. Darrell says his story is about the pressures inside dysfunctional families that drive people to engage in addictive behaviour. Pete agrees with him. Monica doesn't. She doesn't want art to be therapeutic.

Monica got naked with Darrell when Pete went out of town to visit his mother. Monica suspects it won't be long before Darrell tells Pete. Darrell will say he can no longer live with the guilt. He will ensure everyone thinks he is the victim. Darrell is perpetually a victim. Why else would Monica sleep with him?

Monica closes the magazine and walks to the kitchen to get herself a peach.

A large spider plant hangs above the sink. Over the past week small bubbles began appearing in the seams of half a dozen of the long leaves. Monica pointed out the abnormality to Pete (indoor plants are his responsibility) and he tapped his head and said: "Okay. Noted." Upon renewed inspection Monica sees the number of bubbles has increased overnight. She scrapes one off with her fingernail. She supposes it is some sort of bug hidden in some sort of casing. The plant does not look unhealthy, but she supposes it will soon.

When she was a teenager, Monica modelled for a famous sculptor. He stopped her on the street and asked her to sit for him. He later moved to Los Angeles and committed suicide. He sent her a postcard from Big Sur, a postcard of the surf and the cliffs.

For some reason Monica associates Big Sur with Joni Mitchell, and Joni Mitchell with being seventeen. When she was seventeen Monica had a boyfriend who talked about how good things would be when they were married and an uncle who liked to touch her breasts. She used to stand in front of the mirror in her room and undress slowly. She wrote letters about love to her cousin Barbara in Alberta who later became a litigator for an insurance company.

Monica would like to have a baby. She likes to garden. She works part time for an Internet company answering the phone.

Pete first asked to marry her only a month after they met. He had taken her to a hockey game, a photography gallery, a university production of *Waiting for Godot*, and a second-run movie house showing of *The Godfather*. They had not yet slept together. He made it clear he was looking for a wife and three months later Monica saw no reason to turn him down when he asked again. The wedding was on. The in-laws moved in. Wedding plans emerged, solidified, bore fruit in the form of a ceremony, rings, kiss, cake, celebration.

The whole shebang, as Pete often said. The whole big hairy deal.

Monica sits at the kitchen table with her peach and doodles in the margin of the morning paper. She writes a "to do" list in her mind. She has two bills to pay, three emails to answer.

One email is from her friend Gloria in Fredericton. The second is from Gloria's husband David. The third is from her niece Francine in Montréal.

Gloria and David divorced, but then they moved in together again. Gloria is pregnant. They each write regularly to Monica to ask about how to live with the other.

Monica's niece is grieving the death of her hamster. It is her first significant loss. Monica has delayed replying because she wants to be sure to say the right thing, but she fears she may have waited too long to be any kind of support.

Francine is Monica's brother's daughter by his second wife, whose name is Monique. Monique refuses to speak English when Monica visits, which means Monica does not visit often. Monica's brother met Monique when he was in the army stationed in northern Québec. Monica's mother says she knows for a fact that Monique is a separatist. Monica couldn't care less. The way she sees it, Monique is not Cheryl. Cheryl was her brother's first wife. According to Monica, Cheryl was a lunatic; Monique is merely anti-social. Monica's mother is not interested in this distinction. Her father didn't fight in the war so her daughter-in-law could tear the country apart.

"I will do what I have to do for the sake of the children," Monica's mother said to her once.

Monica is confident the country will stay together and her brother's marriage will crumble.

Her brother does not have the profile of a family man. He has a different set of priorities, which is all Monica can claim to know about him. He exists in a world beyond her — a world she has no interest in entering, a world she is sure will one day suck him up piece by piece until there is nothing left of him.

Not a phone number. Not a photograph. Not a memory.

When they were children, Monica, who is three years younger than her brother, followed him around obsessively. Not that he cared — which made Monica obsess about him even more. It wasn't that her brother disliked her. He never abused her, physically or verbally. He simply had no use for her. His indifference was enormous and for the longest time Monica didn't understand it. She thought he hated her or at least felt threatened by her in some way.

It wasn't until she was a teenager that she realized she had been imagining a passion in him that simply did not exist. She sees a connection between her childhood pursuit for her brother's affections and her adulthood acceptance of discreet forms of offered-up love.

The future is clear to her. Her brother will disappear into the echoes of his distant life and she will continue to be a vessel open to the affections of others. This may cost her her marriage.

What will happen when Darrell opens his mouth?

Darrell will trumpet the clarity of his morals. Pete will withdraw into a tight shell of misery. Monica will begin the dual task of nursing Pete back to health and fending off attacks from Darrell's stampeding self-righteous ego.

Will Pete forgive her?

He will ask her for promises she can't keep.

Does she have the courage to lie?

She is not sure she wants to step into the outside world without him, yet there is already a world she goes to that does not include him.

She could say this to him: *I need more space. You're smothering me.* But this is not true. She is happy with what she has; she is happy with Pete.

She is happy with their life together.

Monica is loading the dishwasher when Pete walks in the front door. He has an unlit cigarette behind his ear and a smile on his face. Monica wants to say *Peter, I love you,* but the words won't come. So she meets him in the hallway, grabs him, and holds him, and he squeezes her back.

Something Strange

Audrey Smith licks shut the envelope she's stuffed with thirty-five plastic bread clips. An hour ago she heard a man on the radio trying to collect enough bread clips to get into the *Guinness Book of World Records*. The host invited listeners to help the collector meet his goal.

Audrey sets the envelope on the corner of her bedroom dresser and rushes to put the finishing touches on dinner. Her friend Bill is expected at any minute. She has decided to tell Bill about her dreams.

It all began when she was ten.

"The man who killed the president will die today," she casually told her mother one morning at breakfast. Later, her parents sat her down with a bowl of candy and asked her why she had said what she did, but she pretended not to know.

She has recently dreamed about Bill.

Fifteen years ago, Audrey moved away from Toronto, its expansive university, and the man who wanted to marry her. Bill and his wife, Alissa, were the first people she met. The school board sent them to meet her when her train pulled into Saskatoon.

Audrey left Toronto looking forward to a renewed life on the Prairies, but the first few years passed slowly and were filled with great loneliness. She found her work rewarding, and got satisfaction from leading students on quests for information that would inspire and shape their lives, but she only found real happiness in her deepening friendship with Bill and Alissa, which sustained her. Along with her dreams.

She only dreamed Alissa's death the night it happened. She woke up with her stomach in a knot, tears running down her cheeks. She picked up the phone. Set it back on the receiver. No. She shouldn't call. Her body shook and she gasped. She lifted herself out of bed, walked down the stairs and out into the night. Audrey knelt down and gathered a handful of dirt. She ran her index finger through it. Then cupped her hands together and rubbed the earth through her hair.

Audrey sits cross-legged on the rug, a steaming mug of hot chocolate in her hands. Bill sits in the reclining chair with his legs stretched out in front of him. Audrey has just finished telling him how she first came to know about the images the future deposits in her dreams. She is about to tell him his.

She begins. "You are standing in your garden. The sun is setting. You are watching a pick-up truck approaching you from down the road. The truck leaves a trail of dust behind it. You are thinking about an unpaid debt and the angry man who called you yesterday demanding his money."

Bill's eyes widen.

"The truck pulls into your driveway and cuts across the lawn to where you are standing. A man in a long leather coat gets out of the cab and walks toward you. You exchange a few short sentences, then you are arguing, then fighting. The man knocks you down, kicks you in the head, reaches for a pitchfork — "

"I don't want to hear any more," says Bill.

He stands up and walks into the kitchen. Audrey hears him run himself another glass of water, open the fridge, and drop a few ice cubes into his glass. Ten minutes later he appears, leaning against the doorway, staring at Audrey.

She feels self-conscious and wary.

Bill and Audrey go to bed.

After they are asleep, a flame encircles them. The next day the fire inspectors are puzzled. On the dresser is an envelope, bearing no scars.

Once Upon a Time

He answered the phone. A woman's voice said, "Steve, is that you?"

"Yes."

"It's Noranda."

He raised the palm of his left hand to his forehead. "Where are you?"

"Close to you. At the 7-Eleven."

He named the intersection. "Is that where you are?"

"Yes."

The last time he heard from her — fifteen years earlier — she had sent a letter from Hawaii, where she had been hiding from her manager at a spiritual retreat centre. *I'm pulling myself together*, she had written, and he remembered believing her. He remembered being beyond angry, being beyond hating himself for not being the one who could save her.

He took a beer from the fridge and divided it between two glasses.

He tried to remember the last thing he had read or heard about Noranda. Five years ago she released a come-back album. A world tour followed. He neither bought the album nor attended any of her concerts, but Noranda's face — as photogenic as ever, captured by journalists and television camera crews — had been impossible to ignore. What had she done since? The tabloids had linked her to a television star in California, someone scandalously young for her. She would have been be thirty-eight, he knew, since they were the same age. She had met South African President Nelson Mandela in Cape Town, shared fashion secrets with Princess Diana, and taken a small role in a Hollywood blockbuster that bombed at the box office. Steve had discovered that last fact when he rented the movie to help him through a stolid Saturday night. He had stopped the tape immediately and rewound it. Yes, that's her. Yes, indeed. So she made it to Hollywood at long last. The silver screen had been her first love. Who else but him would know that?

They had grown up together outside of Kingston, not far from the American border. In their small-town high school they had been misfits — not interested in hockey, football, farming, or the proselytizing of the local United Church of Canada Youth Group. Steve was an artist: he sketched, he painted, he took photographs. Noranda wrote music, but no one knew that. The popular girls called her "Mouse," and the boys ignored her. The day of her graduation she travelled to Montréal for a jazz concert and met Steve at the train station. He was heading to Toronto to investigate living arrangements and talk to people at the Ontario College of Art.

"I'm going to U of T in the fall," she said. "Maybe we can live together."

They nested in a sliver of an apartment on College Street, warming quickly to their freedom, the intellectual and emotional growth of post-secondary education, and their growing desire for each other. In the evenings, she would practise her guitar and play her songs for him, and he would encourage her to expand her ambition and perform at local amateur stages. But she always refused. One day, early in their fifth month together, she came to him as he sketched a still life in his room and said she had written a new song — the kind of song that she could record; the kind of song she could give to the world; the kind of song she would *want* to give to the world.

In the fifteen years since he last heard from Noranda, he had thought of her often, but he had talked about her only once. After his divorce, he signed up to take a class in figure drawing. He became popular in his class and started dating one of the models. On their third date, he brought her back to his apartment after an evening at the theatre and they sat up late with a bottle of wine, talking. He was in a nostalgic mood. He tried to identify for the new woman in his life the events that had led him to be with her in that particular apartment, on that particular night, beginning with his upbringing and his refusal to be integrated into his family's stultifying Ontario Protestantism. He had left the Church at fifteen, full of Wordsworthian ambitions to reach the supernatural through art. After high school, he continued on to art college, where he slid into the belly of the post-modern whale. He had lived with Noranda —

"The rock star?" his date asked.

"Yes," he said. "Her. Absolutely."

"You lived with her?"

"Yes," he said. "And I loved her."

On her early tours, he drove the equipment van, talked to reporters, kept a photo album of her private moments. Some of the photos later turned up on her web site. He had come close to demanding royalty payments but decided against it. To him the photos reproduced memories. To others they were part of a mythology, a marketing strategy. What he had, he wouldn't give away. What they already had, they could keep. After her second album, she travelled to Europe. Alone. To gather her thoughts. To write. She felt herself moving in a new direction, she said, though he didn't find out until later that she meant away from him.

In one of the painful moments that followed, he would accuse her of engineering the trauma for her own artistic purposes. She had him barred from her recording sessions, sent her lawyer to their apartment to pick up her possessions. He began a three month booze binge, moved into a basement apartment in Parkdale, and watched as her new album steadily built up sales of 2.5 million copies. Letters began arriving from around the world. Her tour was going well. She missed him. He was the only one who understood her. He wrote, asking for money. She wrote back, calling him a leach.

He slid open the door to his balcony and stepped out to see if he could spot her. His balcony looked out over a minor artery. Traffic was sparse but steady. On the other side of the street the bright light from a television camera suddenly illuminated the sidewalk. Steve saw Noranda standing beside a man with a microphone. He was interviewing her. He couldn't hear what they were saying, but when the man turned and gestured toward his building, he knew they were talking about him.

"You bitch!" he said. He leaned over the balcony and spit. "Hey!" he yelled. "Hey! What do you think you're doing?"

They didn't hear him. He yelled again.

"What do you think you're doing?" He gestured with his arms. "What-do-you-think-that-you-are-do-ing?" He yelled it so loud his throat hurt. He coughed up phlegm and spit again over the balcony. The man with the microphone turned around. Noranda was half-way across the street.

"Stay there!" he yelled. "Stay where you are!"

But she continued across the lawn at the base of his building. The man with the microphone and the man with the television camera followed her.

"Stay where you are!" he yelled again, but they didn't listen.

"It's okay, Steve," he heard Noranda say. "They're with me. They're doing a documentary."

"No shit," Steve said.

Noranda, the man with the microphone, and the man with the television camera huddled beneath his balcony, three floors below him. Noranda tried again.

"It's okay, Steve. It's nothing. Really."

The man with the microphone attempted to be persuasive.

"All we want is a few minutes of your time."

"They want to talk about the early part of my career," Noranda said. "It's for a network special."

The man with the microphone gave the name of the network.

Steve cleared his throat. "I'm not interested."

"Please, Steve."

"No."

"It won't take a minute."

"No."

"Please, Steve."

"No!"

The man with the microphone turned and said something to the cameraman. The cameraman nodded and pointed the camera up at Steve.

"What do you remember about Noranda?" the man with the microphone asked.

"I'm not talking to you," Steve answered.

Three teenagers on skateboards recognized Noranda. They stopped on the sidewalk.

"I'm not talking to you," Steve said again. "I haven't seen Noranda in fifteen years. I have nothing to say, so you might as well go back to where you came from."

"It will only take a minute, Steve," she said.

"The answer is no."

"Steve — "

"No."

"Why not?"

"I'm not interested. I don't want to get involved. You're invading my fucking life!"

Anger swelled out of his pores.

"Once upon a time," he said, resting his hands on the railing. He leaned forward and looked down into the camera. "Once upon a time, I had a sense that my life was going somewhere. Once upon a time, time had a feeling. Time was a dimension. It had depth, texture. It had taste. Once upon a time, Noranda and I had something. Once upon a time, we had something, and what we had, had words. That's about all that I can tell you. We had words for each other, and we don't anymore."

The man with the microphone looked at Noranda.

"You're a jerk, Steve," she said. She turned and walked away from the apartment building. She walked across the lawn and past the skateboarders, who stepped back and didn't ask for her autograph.

Steve watched her go, and smiled.

American Beauty

Another wipe out.

He picks himself up and examines his arm. Blood gathers where he struck the road. It forms into a ball at his elbow and begins a creeping descent to his wrist. He watches it, patient as a soldier awaiting battle, then picks up his bike.

A car rolls to a stop beside him and a old lady calls him to the window. "You all right?" she asks.

He nods.

"You shouldn't be doing tricks like that," she says. "I was watching you as I was coming down the road. I thought you were going to kill yourself."

He looks into her car.

A small dog with a red ribbon around its neck stands on the passenger seat. The dog squeezes out a sickening, sour spark of a yelp.

"I have to get home," he says. He turns his bloody arm towards her. A look of horror floods her face.

"Yes, you better run on home and wash that off. Wash that off and ride safer next time," she stutters.

He spins away from her and mounts his bike.

The blood is down to his hand now, rolling like lava. He wonders if he has thick blood, veins full of sludge.

It comes out so slowly, it must be thick. Like glue holding him together.

As he turns the corner to his street, he notices blood on his leg. He pedals hard to pick up speed, directing his bike like a missile toward the curb.

Watching the Lions

Maury's mother called us the *One-in-Three*. Inseparable, like the Holy Trinity. One organism with three bodies. United in spirit, united in purpose. We shared all things equally: our love of hockey; a taste for vodka; that warm, tight place Maury's sister sheltered between her legs.

For years I did what I could to forget the events of that Sunday afternoon — even when Maury's sister (Gloria was her name) drifted silently out of this world, out of her pain, after swallowing more than the required dosage of her mother's tranquillizers just three days before her sixteenth birthday. I was gone by then, out of town, out of province, studying economics, a set of laws I believed were rational; a set of principles I believed had weathered the storms of time.

Maury informed me of Gloria's suicide in a letter. "I got her diaries," he wrote. "They're gone. Destroyed."

It was the only letter he ever wrote me. For years I hid it with my university papers which I kept stacked in a closet, until I dumped them in a recycling bin five years ago. About to get married, I wanted to rid myself of any evidence of my former life. My former lives.

Maury and I met as children. We lived across the street from each other. Our mothers would pass us back and forth, back and forth, trading diaper duty, nap-time, and mid-afternoon shopping. When I was old enough to walk to school and my mother returned to work, first as a secretary at our parish, and later as a librarian, I would take myself to Maury's for lunch and after-school television. Bob came into our lives a few years later when his family rented a house down the street. His father was a plumber who was perpetually unemployed. His mother worked for the federal government. Bob propelled himself through school on a bevy of scholarships, then landed a tenure track position in the depths of the recession. My mother has never tired of talking about Bob. He had a book out last year about the history of happiness as a philosophical idea. About Maury my mother hasn't spoken in years.

Maury dropped out of high school a month into grade eleven. By then he had a steady income selling and supplying drugs to his friends and junior high kids. He played bass in a band, too, until he tried to organize a coup to remove the singer and found himself tossed out on his ass instead. Our coterie had fallen apart two years earlier. Bob had moved to Toronto to live with his uncle and attend the high school affiliated with the university there.

After Maury dropped out, he hooked up with a punk band from Halifax who needed a driver for their cross-Canada tour. When he turned up on my door step the following summer, sporting a moustache and beard, cigarette in hand and grinning wildly, he looked ten years older.

"I've been to the mountain top," he said. "I have been delivered."

The phrase came from Bob. It had been part of our code. The speaker had gotten laid. The speaker had gotten drunk. The speaker had had a cool time. Listener be jealous.

"Like the mail," I responded. The standard comeback, though the truth was, Maury's reappearance made me uneasy.

The previous week I had run into a girl I knew. Lisa. I ran into her at the mall. She had a job selling popcorn at the cinema. I hadn't seen her in about six months. She had dropped out of school just before the Christmas exams. I thought maybe she had moved away, but when I saw her in the food court sipping coffee she told me a different story. Hadn't I heard? That friend of mine, Maury, had made her pregnant. But Maury hadn't told me. No one had. Maury was known as an easy fuck, and he boasted about many of them, but I had never heard anything about him and Lisa getting together.

"You're a mother?" I asked her.

"No," she said.

The next question never left my lips.

That Sunday afternoon.

Maury's parents were out. We were in their basement. Drinking. Gloria sat watching us. She started wrestling with Maury. He held her down. Then it happened.

It happened.

I used to trace the explosion of our triumvirate to that event. I used to blame that Sunday afternoon, but it wasn't that way. That Sunday afternoon we tried to stop time.

When Maury returned from touring with the punk band, he had a swastika burned into his left forearm. Branded into his flesh.

He made no attempt to hide it.

"It ain't nothin', man," he said. "It's a joke."

We were on our way to a party in Parkdale. I didn't say anything more about it. I didn't believe him.

At the time I had a steady girlfriend named Tina whose parents didn't approve of me because I wasn't Italian, and I hadn't been confirmed. Looking back, my time with Tina was one of the most beautiful periods of my life. I loved to startle her with a kiss on the ear when we sat in movie theatres. She would nibble on my bottom lip when we necked. We spent most of our time together in the library studying, each determined to go to a good university, get a solid education, launch a successful life. We talked about sex, but we didn't do it. It scared me. I simply wanted to be safe with Tina. Away from Maury's darkness. I wanted to be redeemed, purified.

Our relationship survived into the first year of university — until Tina found someone who would sleep with her. She cancelled our dates. She stopped returning my phone calls. Her brother told me the news. I started drinking then, drinking like I hadn't in years. One Friday night I got thrown out of the campus pub for leaping over a chair and arguing with a bouncer. Drunk, I roared into the night, wandered into a residence keg party, and found myself with Jessica, an eighteen-year-old blonde beauty, first on a couch, then gliding down the hall. To her room. Her bed. Her body.

Jessica came from a Westmount family in Montréal. She was studying French literature, but she wasn't doing well in school. She suggested a weekend trip to Florida, and I agreed, but when we got there I couldn't leave our hotel room.

I had a breakdown. Everyone agreed.

"A minor psychotic episode," my doctor said. "Learn to relax."

My parents thought it had to do with Tina. Bob, I think, knew better. He drove out to visit, and we sat in a coffee shop, smoking cigarettes, talking sports.

I threw myself into my studies, did my best to learn the intricacies of supply and demand, a system within which the whole adds up to the sum of its parts.

I met my wife through the first job I had after graduation. I landed a post with an accounting firm. Norma was a painter. Revenue Canada had trawled her tax returns for irregularities, and she came to our firm for help. I met her in the lunch room. She invited me to one of her shows.

She was the first person I told about Gloria. We were into our second year of marriage. Maury was arrested for a murder in British Columbia. I saw the story on the TV news and froze. Norma asked me if something was the matter, and I couldn't respond. I couldn't respond. I froze.

"I know that guy," I said. "We were pals."

I've talked a lot to Norma about what happened. About the way things were. About my guilt, and my feeling of helplessness. When I try now to think about Maury, Gloria, Bob, and myself, I can't focus. I feel like I'm caught in a wind storm, a tornado. Spinning beyond control.

"You're out of it now," Norma says. "You're with me."

She's wonderful and calm, but I'm unable to move on.

Norma and I went to the zoo recently. Every weekend we go for a walk in a different part of the city. Norma takes her camera and snaps images for future paintings. It had been years since either of us had been to the zoo, so I packed a picnic, and Norma loaded a fresh roll of film into her camera. As we stood watching the lions sleeping in their pen, it started to rain.

Norma said she had a dream about Gloria.

In the dream Norma was walking through a park. She came upon a bench. On the bench was a young girl. When Norma approached her, the girl vanished. Norma said she had had this dream three times in the previous week. "I'm thinking of painting her," she said.

"There's a rainbow," I said. It was a big one, broad, beautiful, and deeply hued.

Crow Teaches City Boy
a Few Tricks

"Oi!"
"What?!"
"It's starting."

♎

"Turn up the lights! Strike up the band!"
"No, no. That was last time."

♎

"Last time was different?"
"Last time was the end of the beginning."
"And this time?"
"Is the beginning of the end."

Look, said crow.

I don't see it, I said.

Look, look, said crow.

I said I don't see it, I said. I felt like strangling that bird. We were standing on the southern tip of Manatoulin Island. Me, crow, and the wind. Rain had come and gone. The waves were slow, hard. I was looking for the city, the tower, the dome, the pavement.

Look, said crow.

❧ ☙

Crow said he would teach me things.

Listen to me, city boy, he said.

He had my attention.

The north is the Dark Continent. Forget Africa.

Okay, crow, I said.

I swung my hand and killed a mosquito on my leg.

Good one, said crow.

❧ ☙

Before I met crow it was like this:

The rain on a northern lake fell like lead pellets. I stood beside a pine tree, water pouring over my shoulders. The lake erupted with a million explosions. From the west the rain advanced, beating a front across the lake's dark mirror which absorbed the assault like the devil himself. I unbuttoned my shirt and rolled it off my shoulders. The rain fell. Small rivers sprang up between my toes. The clouds rolled heavily across the sky. The forest roared with the storm. I wiped my hair off my face. A light appeared. The wind blew. The rain slowed to a shower.

Elvis was something, said crow.

Oh, really, I said.

Whole lotta shakin', said crow. He had something I couldn't tell you what. Caught me by surprise, that man did. I used to listen to Sinatra. Then this Presley kid came along. That was something, the first time. Couldn't keep the women still.

     ❧ ❧

I tried to tell crow a joke.

I read a story once, I said.

Yes.

About a girl and three bears.

Goldilocks, said crow.

Yes.

She ate their porridge and slept in their beds.

You know it, then? I asked.

It's quite common, said crow.

I was unaware that bears ate porridge, I said.

Crow laughed so hard he coughed up his lunch.

     ❧ ❧

Crow is a historian and a cartographer.

Have you ever been lost? he asked me.

Yes, sometimes, I said.

Look at that waterfall, he said. Tell me you're not in heaven.

What is today's lesson? I asked crow.

The sun was already high in the sky.

Protecting the nest, said crow.

I'm ready, I said.

Crow let out his magnificent laugh.

Where is your nest, city boy? Where is your nest?

He laughed again and pecked me. Then he flew away.

Speak to the other side of the world, said crow.

I stood up and looked out over the water. I walked to the edge of the rock ledge, put my hands to my face, and prepared to speak. I filled my lungs.

Hello! I yelled.

The word drifted out over the water. We waited as the waves pounded the shore.

I don't think they heard you, said crow.

"The end is still beginning?"
"I think so, yes."

♎

"What I'm trying to ask is: is it over yet?"
"What do you think?"
"Not soon enough."

Acknowledgements

Special thanks to the periodicals who printed some of these stories first, and to everyone at Boheme Press for giving them another life, particularly Max Maccari for his persistence and good humour.

Additional thanks to the Old Testament writers, Thomas Pynchon for *Vineland*, Kurt Vonnegut Jr. for *The Sirens of Titan*, Terry Southern for *Candy*, Raymond Carver for "Neighbors", and Thompson Highway for the introduction to Geoffrey York's *The Dispossessed*.

Along the way the author has been assisted and encouraged by many guides, chief among them Greg Cook, Eric McCormack, and the author's family. Thanks to Northrop Frye for the title, poets everywhere, and to crow for showing the way.